I0684233

Seductive Delights

Sexy Stories Collection

VOLUME 35

10 EROTIC SHORT STORIES

SHALA BREECE

Publisher's Note: This is a work of fiction. Names,
characters, places, and incidents are a product of
the author's imagination. Locales and public
names are sometimes used for atmospheric
purposes. Any resemblance to actual people, living
or dead, or to businesses, companies, events,
institutions, or locales is completely coincidental.

Seductive Delights/ Shala Breece. -- 1st ed.
Xplicit Press, an imprint of TLM Media LLC

ISBN-13: 978-1-62327-566-2
ISBN-10: 1-62327-566-0
eISBN: 978-1-62327-616-4

Printed in the United States of America

CONTENTS

1 THREE'S GREAT COMPANY

It was New Year's Eve and Chris, Monica and Samantha were in a room in one of Miami's most luxurious hotels. Chris lay on the bed watching as the two women locked lips and explored each other's mouths with their tongues.

"Now that's what I'm talking about," he thought. The three of them had been close friends while in college but after graduation they had moved on with their lives, seemingly forgetting about each other. The day when he saw a friend request on Facebook from Monica, his heart leaped with joy, and as he browsed through her profile, he saw another familiar name. Samantha. So without a second thought, he added both women to his friends and wasted no time in reconnecting. Now they were going to reacquaint themselves in a more mature way and private setting.

Chris was jolted from his thoughts by the

sight of the girls slipping each other out of their thin layer of apparel. Monica's red lace tube dress was the first to fall to the floor, exposing her delicious looking chocolate brown skin. She wore a red lace thong that matched her outfit along with a sheer red stocking. His eyes carefully examined every inch of her almost naked body as his desire for her increased instantaneously. His dick throbbed in anticipation of the feel of her chocolate flesh. He had always been attracted to Monica in college but since she had been dating his friend at the time, it would have been inappropriate to express his feeling towards her. Sam's dark spandex mini dress also crumbled to the floor allowing him the pleasure of seeing her lily-white skin. Her skin tone was the exact opposite of Monica's which made this whole experience all the more exciting for him. Being a Caucasian man, he was constantly fucking other Caucasian women, and it was not because he particularly wanted to. But every time he had tried to speak to or date a woman of color, she would always turn him down.

"Suck her tits, Sam," he begged as he looked on.

There was no hesitation on her part; she immediately took hold of Monica's melon shaped breast and moved her mouth from the right nipple, and then to the left. Monica moaned as she tilted her head backwards, popping out her chest a little. Sam's hand ran wildly over her body and he could feel his dick increasing in size as he looked on. He had to swallow hard when he saw Sam clasp teeth on

Monica's nipple and gently pull on it. Monica gave a soft shriek, but he could not tell whether it was from the pain of the pressure of having Sam's teeth biting her nipples, or whether it was from the pleasure that followed when she gave the nipple a long gentle suck. With her lips pleasuring Monica, Sam used her hand and traced downwards from her breast to her navel, her hand finally stopping at its destination between her thighs.

"Damn you girl, you're so wet." Sam said.

She pulled her fingers out of the small space between Monica's body and the thong that she was wearing. Her fingers glistened with a delicious looking liquid that she had extracted from Monica's pussy. She looked straight ahead at Chris and licked her fingers. The thought of tasting Monica's pussy for himself had him hornier than both the girls realized. He whipped out his long golden brown dick, and began stroking it with the palm of his hand. Sam returned her hand down between Monica's thigh and she was plunging her fingers violently in and out of her wet pussy Monica could hardly remain balanced as Sam used her fingers to fuck her pussy. As Chris looked on, he realized that he could cum by just watching this but that would mean that he would not get to fuck Sam so he decided to make another demand.

"Stop Sam," he ordered, in a firm voice that caught both women off guard. "I wanna see you handle what you've been dishing out," he said, giving them a wicked little smile.

Both women had been so engrossed in each other that they had forgotten that he was even in the room. They quickly changed positions and Sam found herself at the receiving end of Monica's hot wet tongue. Her nipples were rock hard and Monica tugged and pulled at them while holding onto her body to ensure that she kept her balance. Sam's white thong was ripped away and tossed to the corner of the room. Chris's dick shot up to an even harder degree of erection as nearly cracked under the pleasure of seeing the two women getting it on. Clearly, the women liked what they were doing. He had not expected things to quite turn out the way it was. In fact, he did not think that they would have been so open to his idea of them having some foreplay while he watched, but yet here they were, enjoying each other's body.

Monica went down on her knees and gave Sam two soft taps on her knee, motioning her to part her legs. A loud moan escaped Sam's lip as Monica swept through her wet pussy with her hot tongue. Chris made a noise at the sight of the Monica eating Sam's pussy out. With her legs parted, Sam's body jerked back and forth, as Monica's tongue caressed her pink pussy lips. Another moan, and with his dick in his hand, he bent his head slight to the left to get a better view of the pussy action going on before him. His eyes caught sight of Monica's mouth stretching and pulling on Sam's clitoris. Monica continued to eat Sam's pussy in long strokes.

Finally, Chris had had enough. He called out to the girls and invited them to join him on the large king sized bed.

Monica took a little while before she released Sam. Then they made their way over to the bed. Realizing how horny Sam was as a result of his interruption, he decided to continue the job Monica had been doing on her pussy. She was all too thrilled and bent over at the top of the bed, directly over his face, allowing him complete access into the insides of her thighs. Monica too, being the amazing cocksucker that she was decided to give Chris a taste of her wicked tongue on his large, hardened dick. When she took his dick into her mouth, he was forced to release Sam's clitoris for a while and look down at her in amazement. He could understand why Sam had wanted more of her tongue. She was an expert. Again, she gave his dick another long hard suck and then nibbled her lips over his head. Jolts of pleasure sped through his body as he tried to focus his attention on sucking Sam's dripping, wet pussy.

Monica did not caress the dick much; she was more of an intense dick sucker. He could feel her tongue lavishing his dick with sensuous strokes and hard long sucks. A flick at the head, and another hard suck. Again, and again, he felt her hot tongue, sucking his hard member. He almost felt like he would explode in her mouth at any minute. As he flicked his tongue around in Sam's pussy, the pleasure he was receiving from Monica's tongue must have been running through his body and now transferring via his tongue into Sam's pussy. He found it hard to control the jolting and the sudden jerks that Sam was giving against his mouth.

He gripped onto the top of her hip area, and plunged his tongue all the way up into her pussy. She moaned out, begging him not to stop, but he was not about to release her from his lips anytime soon. His tongue continued to work its way in and out of her wet pussy. He was also occasionally taking hold of her clitoris with his mouth and sucking it with long hard pulls, the way Monica was sucking his dick. Monica had now intensified his pleasure by taking hold of his tender balls and caressing them with her hand. Her tongue released his dick and made its way to his balls. He gasped as she sucked his balls into her mouth.

Chris had never experienced anything like this before and he was trying hard to control himself. He found himself wanting to feel Sam's pussy on his dick but he knew that he would feel cheated if he did not get an opportunity to fuck Monica as well. His tongue left Sam's pussy and it took all his strength to pull away from Monica's firm grip on his dick. This caused a brief interruption in their little ménage-trios. They decided to switch things up a little and kick it up a notch. Monica now found herself lying down on the bed, with Sam bent over between her legs, and Chris in the back of Sam ready to fuck her from behind. Sam's tongue moved inside Monica's delicious chocolate brown pussy. The intriguing thing about Monica's pussy was it was chocolate brown on the outside yet the inside was pretty pink. Monica was moaning out in pure ecstasy as Sam ravished her inch by inch with her expert tongue.

Chris had been trying hard to control his strokes because he wanted to save some of himself for Monica but it was getting harder and harder by the minute. As he thrust his huge cock inside Sam's pussy she jerked forward, and her tongue dug deeper into Monica's pussy. It made Chris feel like Monica was receiving pleasure from the impact of his strokes. His thoughts were distracted from Monica as he felt Sam's juices oozing out onto his dick. He grabbed hold of her petite white ass and fucked her as hard as he could. This would be a night that he did not want either woman to forget. Harder and harder he went, and the fact that she was now grinding her ass against his dick with every thrust was driving him insane. He pulled out trying to catch his breath and prevent his ejaculation. But her pussy had been so warm and inviting that he could not stay out of it for long. Monica moaned and begged as Sam worked harder on her pussy.

Chris looked on as Sam continued to indulge her tongue in Monica's pussy. The feel of Sam's tongue must have been unbearable, as Monica clenched her teeth and her body twisted and turned from left to right. She grabbed the sheets that had she had been knotting in her fingers and placed it between her clenched teeth. His heart thudded and he instantly found himself shoving his dick back with full force into Sam's wet pussy. He gripped unto her ass, and with some hard thrusts he exploded inside her. His loud groan was mixed with Monica's loud moans as she came into Sam's devouring mouth. His cum was hot and dripping out of Sam's pussy. She looked back at him and gave him a warm smile that let him know that she had been fully satisfied by his dick.

The three of them lay in the bed next to each other with Chris in between the two women. A short time later, they were all awakened by the sound of people on the streets making noise and welcoming the New Year, with fireworks and booming music. As Chris got out of the bed, he walked over to the window. The view was amazing from the twenty-first floor of the high-rise hotel and they could see the entire city from the small patio area. The two women followed closely behind him wearing nothing but their thin layer of underwear. He turned around and saw the two almost naked females in his presence. His dick shot up as he watched the moonlight hit their beautiful soft skin and flashes of their pleasure began running through his mind. Then it hit him, mid-way in his thoughts that he had not been able to hold on and had ejaculated before even getting an opportunity to fuck Monica. Although she was not bothered by it because she had gotten her release on Sam's tongue, he could not get it out of his mind. He needed to fuck Monica; it had been a dream of his from the time they were in college.

After the fireworks, the three made their way back to the bed, and conveyed the same thought without even saying a word to each other. It was time for round two. This time Chris found himself back on the bed with Monica on top riding his dick, while Sam was further at the top bent over with her pussy making direct contact with his waiting mouth. He gobbled her up with his mouth and stuck his tongue in and out of her tender swollen pussy. He gently caressed her tender flesh as if trying to make up for the harsh pounding he had given it hours earlier. Sam gave out loud moans that sounded almost like she was singing. She had her hands over her huge breasts fondling them while biting her lips and enjoying his tongue working the insides of her pussy.

The entire night Chris had had a hard time trying to control his attention. Even as he was trying to pleasure Sam, his attention was captured by the feel of Monica's tight wet pussy riding up and down his dick. She was bouncing on his dick with such vigor and force that it seemed like he would explode inside her at any time. Her pussy was hot and warm and she bobbed up and down and then rocked from side to side, whispering profanities at him while fucking him. She was truly a wild woman at heart, even with this huge dick inside her tiny pussy she had managed to pull it off like a boss. The entire time Monica had been fucking him at her own pace and he found it increasingly hard to just lay back and enjoy the ride. He finally gave in to the desire, and grabbed her firmly, securing her wet pussy on his dick and began fucking her in return, thrusting upwards. She shrieked out at the feel of his long dick inside her. A small wicked smiled escaped from the corners of his lip as his eyes lit up. Now he had total control over her.

"Oh Chris, shit!" she moaned as he fucked her pussy with his mighty upwards thrusts.

Her body slammed hard against his with every thrust. She stretched outwards with her palms on his chest, tilting her head backwards in an attempt at taking control of the situation. He found her grinding hard against him and he could feel his dick hitting every wall inside her pussy. His dick throbbed at the new sensations that were now jolting through his body, and then he almost lost it when he felt her lean downwards, and put her hot wet tongue on his nipples.

"Oh fuck yeah," he groaned as he pulled briefly away from the insides of Sam's thighs.

Monica had now found his secret g-spot, and was caressing and sucking his nipples. He felt like he would lose his mind and he increased the heat on Sam's pussy. He pushed his hand upwards and found her pussy lips. He used his thumb and forefinger and rubbed onto her swollen clitoris as he ravished the inside of her pink flesh.

Monica fucked his cock with her wet pussy while flicking her wet tongue back and forth and around his tender nipples. Chris felt a sudden rush of blood run through his body and his hot liquid shot upwards inside of

Monica's pussy. He increased the momentum of the strokes of his tongue inside Sam's pussy causing her to climax along with Monica. The two women collapsed with exhaustion on the bed next to him and the three of them dozed off.

Chris was awakened by the sound of Sam's stilettos on the marble tile in their hotel room. He looked at her, in black dress pants and a white blouse with her hair neatly tucked in a ponytail and thought how just looking at her one would never be able to tell that she had had such a wild night.

"Wow, you're up early," he said rubbing his eyes, while slowly seating upwards on the bed. He looked around the room for Monica but she was still under the sheets.

"Yeah, I want to go visit some of my cousins before I head back to Chicago, tomorrow." Sam replied, as she applied a shade of pink lipstick in a round mirror on the wall directly in front of the bed.

"Well I had a great time last night." Chris said as he stood up and walked across to where she had been standing to give her a goodbye hug.

Sam smiled and replied, "I had a great time too," before exiting the room.

Chris took a deep breath and made his way back to the bed to continue his early morning nap. As he lay in the bed, he realized that this was a great opportunity for him to get some one-on-one time with Monica. He gently pulled back the sheets that she had used to cover her naked body. As he looked at her sleeping form, he remembered how he was once infatuated with her. She was so beautiful, and he was especially in love with her chocolate complexion. In fact, chocolate was his favorite delicacy. Her breasts were full and firm, and her nipples were perfectly round and inviting. He could not resist; he moved in closer to her and gently took one of her nipples into his mouth. As he sucked her nipple, the rest of her body gradually began to come alive. He sucked it long and hard, nibbling his mouth over her nipples. She was now moaning with her eyes closed, clearly she must have thought that she was dreaming.

His dick throbbed as the desire to fuck her became more and more intense. When he could no longer control himself, he mounted her and penetrated her already wet pussy with his hard dick. Her eyes popped open at the feel of her pussy being filled. A soft moan escaped her lips when she realized that she was not dreaming. His dick had been craving her pussy for years and when it finally felt her moistness, it was difficult to control himself. He heard her say something about his dick was the longest dick she had ever had. Her compliment made him cockier than he already was, and he began to increase the momentum of his thrust. His huge dick rammed her insides and sent shockwaves of pleasure through their bodies. He had his lips locked onto her nipples, caressing them with his hot, wet tongue. The air was filled with her moans and his panting, as they fucked each other for what seemed like hours.

Chris could feel her hot liquid all over his dick and it made it even harder to control him. Her pussy was sweet and dripping wet.

"I'm gonna fucking cu...!" he said, but before he could finish his statement, he exploded his hot cum inside her equally aroused pussy. Her body quivered as she too let out a loud moan and reached her orgasm. They fell back in each other's arms and tried to recover from all their fucking that they had done.

This would be a good year, Chris thought to himself with a smile. But he could not help wonder what it would have felt like with Sam there to increase the pleasure. The more he thought about it the more he wanted to see Sam again. In fact, he wanted to see both Sam and Monica together again. Although sometimes three could be a crowd, having the two of them there, with their wet cunts just waiting to be licked and fucked was an amazing experience.

He picked up his phone and dialed Sam's number in hopes that she would accept his offer to meet again tonight. However, this time he would be more prepared for the two women, now that he had seen what they were capable of doing in bed. When she did not pick up, he left her a voicemail "Hey Sam, you busy tonight? Wondering if we can get back together, you, me and Monica." He rolled over to where Monica had been lying naked and gently planted a soft kiss on her pink lips. Then he got up and tried to recover from the long night he had had with the two women. Yes, he thought, three was definitely good company.

2 GANGSTER'S DELIGHT

"**O**rder up!" Olivia Lewis said jokingly to the chef who had to take over for her that night. The chef barely glanced up as she exited out the back door.

Her car had been down for a few months now, and she was forced to use public transportation. As she made her way through the narrow alley, she could not help but feel like she needed to increase her pace, as there was something different about tonight.

Her heart thudded as she walked faster, almost at the point of running. Suddenly, out of nowhere, a firm masculine hand grabbed her by her throat, the other hand securing his palm as a barrier on her mouth. Her hand automatically lifted to grip his arm, and she pulled, hard. A shriek escaped the lips of her attacker, and someone else grabbed her hands. Her purse fluttered to the ground with a soft pat. She heard it scrape as one of the men picked it up. She ran toward the light, and one of their faces caught her eye. He held her purse, and she tried to scream as he ran away. Then, out of the darkness, the figure of a man flew past her, heading in the direction of the thieves.

"Let her purse go," he yelled.

His voice was deep, sort of like the rumble of thunder. She looked on curiously, as the men engaged in a brief struggle. He had caught up with the no-good thugs and had one in a headlock while the other scuffled away in fear. He snatched her purse out of the would-be thief's hands and spoke to him in a soft deadly tone. Olivia moved closer to where the action was, hoping to catch a glimpse of the face of her Good Samaritan. He finally released the helpless assailant from his tight grip, and the man promptly ran away. He turned to face her and she felt taken aback by his lean physique. He was well built and very attractive, with a dark edgy look to him. He stretched out his hand, her recovered purse dangling from it.

"Thank you so much!" she exclaimed, her green eyes staring at his face. Her curious face had relaxed a bit, as she examined this mysterious stranger, inch by inch with her eyes.

He gazed back at her with a smile and she noticed his entire bad boy demeanor. He had an earring in his left ear and a tattoo of a tiger on his left shoulder.

"It was no problem, I can see that you're still shaken up, can I offer you a ride home?" he asked, pointing to a black corvette in the distance.

She smiled and nodded at him, "Yes please."

She could not help but notice the cologne, which clung to the shirt he draped around her shoulders to keep her warm. She also noticed the other tattoo of the cross on his right shoulder.

He held the door open for her to get in and she murmured her thanks. She realized that she was attracted to him and a wicked thought came across her mind. She had always had fantasized about being with a gangster and as she sat in the front seat of his car, it felt like her dream was about to come to fruition. Her thoughts were interrupted by the sound of the engine, as he started the car, and drove off into the night. They introduced themselves and soon engaged in lively conversation. There was an undeniable chemistry between them.

His name was Terrence and he told her that he worked as a bouncer in a club about a block down from the restaurant where she worked. He stopped at a red light and he looked at her. Her brown hair flowed over her shoulders, and she had naturally pink lips. She wore no makeup, he noticed. Her round face and high cheekbones looked heavenly. He had never felt what he was feeling at this exact moment. It took all of his willpower to prevent himself from ripping all her clothes off right then and there. As they sat there in the few seconds waiting for the light to change color, he felt her soft touch on his hand; she was thanking him again for retrieving her stolen purse. The look that he gave her in response to her touch was all she needed. She leaned over to his seat, and in an instant unzipped his fly. She had never done this before, but felt it was appropriate for that moment.

She whipped out his huge dick and began stroking it with her hand. Then she placed her hot desire filled tongue on the tip of the head. Her tongue caressed the entire length of his erect dick, causing him to accelerate on the gas pedal. She licked and sucked every inch of his dick, and his groans were loud and thunderous as they speed through the traffic. Every lick was more intense than the previous one, and she found herself using her mouth to go up and down on his huge cock.

Terrence tried his best to not lose control of the car. Finally, he pulled up in a dark parking lot next to two other parked cars. His eyes carefully surveyed their surroundings, then with a click he locked the doors. Somewhat more secure inside, he made his way to the back seat, motioning her to join him. Her breath caught in her throat as he gently tugged onto in her bottom lip with his soft, full lips. His tender kisses sent shockwaves through her body, as her juices saturated her lace thong. His large hands cradled her face as she slipped her hands underneath his shirt. Her hands explored his chest and he popped one button on her blouse. Her white lace bra and nipples showed all too well. She gasped as he took out one full breast and sucked on it while his other hand slipped under her skirt. She passed her shirt over her head and unhooked her bra, her breath growing raspy as she did so. Her bra dropped down and he unhooked his belt. He whispered obscenities in her ear as he pulled his pants down.

She lay naked, and when he slipped his hands upwards into her moist heat, she moaned from the sensation of his touch. His index finger explored her insides over and over, and soon she felt a second finger inside her, and then a third. He used all three fingers to penetrate her tender insides over and over again. He gradually increased the pace of his finger thrusts inside her. Suddenly he stopped; he was no longer satisfied with just finger fucking her. He stroked his dick and then positioned her in the back seat parting her legs before propping them up in the air. Her pussy went down on his dick, like chocolate syrup on ice cream.

"How can such an innocent looking girl can have such a sweet, wicked pussy," Terrence wondered, and felt his control slowly slipping away. Her pussy was wet, and hot, and she was grinding and bouncing it against his dick. He could see that she was enjoying herself. He went inside her pussy deeper and Olivia begged him for more. She was in pure ecstasy; she licked her lips over and over and kept her eyes shut as she focused her attention on enjoying every minute of their experience. The more he fucked her, the harder it seemed to maintain control of the situation; he was now fucking her with his eyes closed while whispering profanity to peak her arousal. She increased her momentum, slamming her wet pussy on his dick as she rocked back and forth after every impact. He took her swollen, hard, round nipples in his mouth, sucking it with long, wet, gentle pulls.

As the sensations increased, he gripped her ass and thrust his dick harder inside her pussy. She shrieked with pleasure at the feel of his active participation. They both began to devour each other's lips, gasping in pleasure. With one last hard thrust, his hot liquid shot up inside her, and they both climaxed; their bodies quivered under the intensity of their explosion. They quickly put their clothes back on, and then he cranked the car and drove her home.

He parked the car at the side of the street and she looked at him thankfully. He gazed into her eyes and leaned forward involuntarily, to give her a good-bye kiss. As their lips met once more, the flames of desire that they had felt at parking lot were once again ignited. Their tongues engaged in a series of hot wet passionate kisses. When she finally broke free from his grip, she could feel her wet pussy wanting more. It had not been an hour since they last fucked and here she was again, more horny than before. She knew exactly what he had to offer and wanted more. She tried to control herself, getting out of the car in order to make a quick exit before her feeling got the best of her.

"Wait, why are you leaving?" he asked, and gestured towards her open shirt, which she had forgotten to button.

She glanced at him, and could not help smiling like an idiot. His shirt was unbuttoned revealing a mane of ruffled chest hair, and his pants, without a belt, were falling to the driveway, where they stood. Her house lay in complete darkness, and all her neighbors were already in bed. What the hell, she figured, this was the first and last time she would some strange guy over in the late hours of the night. "Why don't you come in for a drink?" She asked and made a deliberate attempt at fixing her hair. He had ignited a feeling inside her that she could not extinguish. She was hot, and right now, they both knew what would cool them down. He nodded and she led the way, ignoring the bells that were tingling, warning her against him a second time

When she entered the house, she felt his presence fill the air. His warmth circulated and she felt safe. She held his hand and guided him to the couch. He took her hand and they sat down. There was no time for chatting or drinks, their lips locked together, once more, and their hands ran wild over each other's bodies, fingers practically ripping each other's clothes off. Once they were completely naked, he gently laid her down on her huge leather couch. She gulped for air as he teased her, putting himself in between her thighs, pleasuring her with his hot tongue. He took his time caressing, and sucking her clit. She moaned out in pleasure, calling out his name begging him to suck it and lick her harder.

He had never been one to follow instructions, but in this case he was willing to make an exception. His tongue glided up and down her moist flesh, working its way inside the narrow opening, and wiggling a little. She moaned out even louder this time. He sucked her pussy like she had offered him some sweet delicacy and he was now indulging in it. His hand found its way inside her thighs and his fingers stroked against her tender flesh, while his tongue caressed her clitoris. She felt like she would lose her mind; she whimpered at the feel of his finger and his tongue pleasuring her at the same time.

"Oh God you're going to drive me crazy," she shrieked, as she tried to push her pussy backwards away from his tongue.

But he would not have it, he grabbed onto her with such force that a small scream escaped her mouth, then he had her right back in the previous position while he began to gently nibble on her clitoris.

Olivia longed to feel Terence's huge dick inside her. Using his hand, he stroked his erect dick, before gently thrusting it inside her wet pussy. She moaned a little as his dick slowly penetrated her insides.

"Oh shit, yeah, fuck" he groaned, as he pushed his dick inside her pussy.

As he thrust inside her warm core, once again, he pulled out and carefully examined the look on her face. He leaned in and planted a soft gentle kiss on her forehead. For some reason, he felt very affectionate towards her. He did not want her to feel much pain, only sheer pleasure. She held onto him as he entered her slowly. The way he stroked her pussy brought about a sweet pleasurable feeling. She closed her eyes while a loud moan escaped her desire-filled lips. He groaned as he shifted inside her and she cried out unable to do anything else.

Being the gangster that he was he decided to switch positions a little. He also knew a thing or two about how to please a woman, using the right positioning. Terrence gently pulled his dick out of her pussy and positioned her on the couch for the next couple of thrusts. He knelt down in front the couch while she slouched back with her legs parted and up in the air. He pushed her leg backwards as his dick found its way inside her wet pussy. She moaned out loud; she could feel every inch of his dick as it penetrated deep down inside her pussy. He gave her some long, hard thrusts, and then the momentum of his thrusts increased as he came closer to his climax. They had also found a rhythm with each other, every thrust caused her to jolt back a little and as he fucked her, Olivia began to come in long pulsing waves.

The intensity of his thrusts continued to increase, and he now was now viciously pounding her pussy with quick, hard thrusts.

They sent small moments of pain into Olivia but there was a hint pleasure in it. Her body shuddered with every hard slam, and the sound of his balls on her ass penetrated though their moans. Tiny spasms ran from the back of her spine all the way down to the tip of her clitoris

"Yes, yes, oh God, yes," she moaned out loud as she reached her shuddering climax.

Terrence gripped her tightly as he gave her some long hard strokes, followed by some quick harder slams. He lets out a loud groan as he exploded his hot cum inside her accommodating pussy before the two of them fell back in each other's arms as they tried to collect themselves.

They had tried to cuddle to gather on the couch, but the couch only had space for one person.Deciding to let him stay the night, she led him upstairs to her room. It's the least she could have done, he had pleased her in so many ways the least he deserved is a good place to lay his head for the rest of the night. He laid her down on one side of the bed exhausted and held onto her hot sweaty body as they dozed off together.

The next morning she woke up and the lump on the bed next to her proved why she felt all hot and bothered. He rolled over and she could clearly see his body as the sun pierced through the blinds. "He must be one of those guys that wake up with a hard on,"

she thought, noticing the way his dick stood at attention. His dick was so tempting she just could not conceal her desire to suck it. Slowing bringing her lips to the tip of its head, she licked at his hard dick.

Terrence opened his brown eyes to find Olivia's mouth running wild all over his dick from the head to the base, sucking and licking it with an amazing rhythm. He groaned and swallowed hard, trying to find the strength to speak. They had fucked twice the night before and now he was awakened by the feel of her hot wet tongue on his dick. He could definitely see himself walking up to her lips on his in the future. He pulled his dick away from her mouth for a brief minute and sat up to give her a lingering kiss on the forehead.

She gave him a wicked little smile as she cupped his dick in the palm of her hands.

"Good morning," he said as he kissed her, and trailed hot wet kisses down her breasts. Her nipples were hard, and he gently caressed each one with his tongue. He sucked and licked her hard nipples and she moaned to his touch. He slowly moved his attention down to her tummy and spent a few lingering minutes there, using his tongue to tease her sensitive spots. She moaned out loud, and in a desire-filled voice, she begged him to fuck her, telling him that she needed it inside her now.

This woman was just blowing his mind away; she was waking him up with blowjobs and begging for his dick inside her. Without warning, he gripped his manhood and fondled it until he gave a growl that sounded animal like. She slid down his full length, gliding her wet pussy down his erect dick then she rocked her pussy back and forth on his dick, making him groan out loud, calling her name. He was normally not good with names, but she was an exception, he definitely knew her name, he had been calling it out all night. "Olivia, Olivia, sweet Olivia" he thought to himself as her pussy drove him crazy.

He tried hard to control his impending ejaculation but her pussy was like a sweet magnet and the more he tried to control himself, the more he was actually losing control. She herself could feel a climax around the corner and began to arch her hips harder before pulling up off his dick, and then slamming her pussy back down the entire length of it, giving a loud moan as she reached her climax. He was not far behind with his explosion of cum either. The two reached sweet ecstasy as they collapsed on the bed exhausted from it all.

He arrived downstairs five minutes later, fully dressed, and looking more handsome than ever. In his hand, he held a paper, which he laid carefully on the counter with a black pen.

"Can I call you? Because I had a great time last night," he whispered, and she smiled. She wrote the number down on the paper and handed it back to him. He tore a small piece from the paper, and wrote his name and number on it, before handing it to her. He left her with a passionate kiss and he was out the door promising to call her. As soon as his black corvette rumbled away, she leaned back against the stainless steel fridge wondering what had just happened. Last night was the best night of her life, and she was greatly surprised by his gentleness. But whatever was going on between them had ended when she had reluctantly left the bed just a measly ten minutes ago. She was not convinced that he would call.

"But who knows? He might just surprise me." She said and heard the sound of her cell phone ringing the distance. She searched the room eagerly, in hopes that it might be Terrence. Her hopes were a bit crushed when she heard her best friend on the other end of the call. She soon began telling her about her encounter with this gangster. Her intrigued friend laughed at first, but then urged her to call Terence.

She got off the phone and flipped her laptop open, turning it on. She went to her video archives and clicked on her favorite porno, "Gangster's Delight." As she sat there, watching the huge chocolate man in the video ram his dick over and over in the petite blonde woman, she could feel herself getting aroused. Her wetness saturated her panties, and she soon found herself using her fingers to pleasure her moist pussy. The video reminded of the way Terrence had fucked her during the last couple of hours. She rammed two of her fingers in her pussy, rubbing against her clitoris with her thumb. As the man in the video gave his final hard thrust she also climaxed, her finger was now wet with her ejaculation. She calmed herself from her brief moment of pleasure, and quickly searched through her the draws in her kitchen to find the piece of paper with Terrence's number on it. When she found it, breathed a sigh of relief, and flipped her cell phone open, eagerly dialing his telephone number. After a few rings, a familiar rugged male voice answered the call. It was Terrence. She felt butterflies in her stomach as her she nervously prepared to ask him out on a date.

3 A SUGAR DADDY FOR LISA

"I 'll get the bill", Tony said.

He pulled out his black leather wallet and removed his credit card. He placed the card with the bill on a small tray and signalled the waiter to come over to their table. Lisa could not believe her eyes, it was a very rare day when her boyfriend Tony paid for anything at all. He just didn't have the means.

When she had met him, he had said that he was trying to find a job that suited him; a year later he was still very much unemployed. She had been practically supporting him on her very small minimum wage salary. However, that night when he paid for the dinner that he had invited her to, she was left wondering whether he had secretly gotten a job, and if he had, why had he not told her? Lisa decided that she did not want to ask too many questions and ruin their romantic evening so she sat quietly and watched him pay for the expensive meal they had just enjoyed.

He used his firm masculine hands as a blindfold against her eyes as he opened the door to their bedroom. They made their way into the room, and when they were half way inside, he slowly removed his hands over her eyes. A look of amazement came across her face as a loud gasp escaped her soft lips.

"You did this for me," she said as she looked around at the beautiful, candle-decorated room.

The sweet scent of the burning candles almost intoxicated her. His hand gently cupped her face as he brought his lips down to meet hers. Lisa was swept away in the sensations of his tender kiss, and tiny waves of ecstasy made their way down the middle of her back and to the core of her womanhood. Their tongues engaged in a lengthy passionate kiss while their mouths moved from left to right, as if trying to devour each other. When their lips parted, Lisa felt his tongue making its way down to her round hard nipples. As his mouth took hold of her nipple, she moaned loud and used her hand on the back of his head to pull him in closer to her flesh. He stroked her gently with his tongue, and she moaned as she enjoyed the hot wetness on her nipples. He must have read her mind because his next move was exactly what she had been hoping he would do.

Picking her up gently in his strong, chocolate-hued arms, he placed her on their feather soft bed. His hand gently rolled her short red lace dress upwards to her black lace thong. His tongue was hot, almost like fire. As he traced his way upwards between her thighs, she begged him desperately to eat her pussy. Using his teeth, he pulled down her thong all the way down to her ankles and dove his head back upwards to her clean-shaved pussy. Lisa almost lost her mind the moment she felt his hot tongue land inside her wet cunt. He certainly did not waste any time. He used his tongue and stroked the insides of her pussy, flicking it all over her clitoris. Lisa's fingers dug into the white satin sheets that had been neatly spread on the bed, but were now ruffled from movements while in ecstasy. His tongue worked its way, back and forth, in and out of her wetness. She could feel her juices running down her body with such intensity that she wanted to scream out and let the entire world know how good she felt. And she did let out a loud scream, when he suddenly gripped unto her clit with his teeth. Now that he had her clit in his mouth, he used that opportunity to rub his tongue against it in small circular motions.

He seemed to be enjoying some delicious meal because he latched on to her pussy with an even greater force, and the gentle small circular motions on her clit became harder fast flicks. With his tongue keeping her at the peak of her arousal, he penetrated her with two of his long fingers. First, he used his fingers to gently stroke the insides of her pussy, and then, his gentle strokes turned into vicious jabs. He was thrusting them in and out of her pussy; his fingers now well lubricated with her the clear liquid that was flowing out. He finally released her pussy from his mouth and looked deep into her desired-filled eyes. Her hair was a mess from her running her fingers wildly through it while he had been devouring her pussy.

As their eyes met, he slowly rose up from between her legs and unzipped his pants, whipping out his big dick. She sat up and came closer to him, while he was now in a kneeling position on the bed. She gently caught hold of his erect dick and brought her mouth to it, giving it a long gentle suck. He took a deep breath as she continued to suck his huge dick, running her tongue over it and then flicking it at the tip. His dick was long, with a small curve in its structure, close to the head. She sucked and sucked his cock, and when he felt like he was about to explode, he pulled his dick away from her hungry mouth. He must have thought that it would be better to climax inside her pussy, because he immediately penetrated her wet cunt with his hardened dick.

He had bent her bent over, on her hands and knees with her ass propped up, waiting to receive him. Lisa felt him use his hands to part her ass cheeks as his dick made it way downwards in search of her tight pussy whole. It hardened a bit, when it made contact with her the wetness of her juices. He groaned a little as he used his dick to tease her pussy a little, stroking around the edge of her opening. Without warning, he slammed his long dick inside her pussy, causing her insides to shudder at the force of his impact.

He must have gotten a high from fucking

her hard and rough because the next set of thrusts seemed somewhat unbearable for Lisa. Then he stopped and slowed down a little thrusting inside her with less force. He had switched up his style of fucking and was now giving her long slow thrusts, each time pulling his dick out of her pussy, almost at its head and then gently thrusting the dick back inside her. Lisa moaned in ecstasy, and found herself calling out his name begging him to fuck her harder.

"Oh, you want me to tear that pussy up, okay," he said with a wicked smile on his face.

He gripped firmly unto her ass, and braced himself for the hard fuck that she had just begged for. He slammed his huge dick with all his might inside her pussy.

"Oh gosh!" she shrieked as she tried to move forward to easy the intensity of his thrusts.

It was no use. He grabbed onto her ass even tighter than before and gave her several quick hard thrusts, each one harder and faster than the last. Lisa could feel her climax nearing and she sank her teeth into the pillow in front of her, like an animal into its prey. Over and over, he rammed his hard long cock inside her pussy.

"Oh, oh, oh...shitttttttttttt!!!!!!" Tony cried and shot his hot liquid all up inside her wet cunt.

Lisa found herself reaching her climax, and closed her eyes, as she exploded her liquid onto his waiting dick.

Later, while they lay in the bed cuddling in each other's arms, he asked her to lend him some money so that he could purchase a car. That smart bastard, she thought as she lay there. How could she say no to him, when he had just given her one of the best orgasms of her life? After thinking about his request for a minute, she told him that she would lend him the money by the next evening.

Lisa opened her eyes and looked around the room; the clock showed that it was seven o'clock. She rushed out of bed fearing that she would not make it in time for her eight o'clock shift at the restaurant. As she headed to the bathroom, she could hear Tony's voice in there singing off-key as usual; just when she was about to go rush him out of the shower, she realized that his phone had been blinking from the time she had first opened her eyes. With her curiosity getting the best of her, she flipped the phone open to see why it was blinking. The next thing that caught her eye sent ripples of shock and anger through her body. There were text messages sent to and from a mysterious contact labeled "sweetie", and it was definitely not any of her numbers. As she browsed through the phone, the second most recent text message was the most offensive to her.

"Boy, when is you bringing that cock over here? Hope u didn't have to sleep with that whore to get the money for our car."

She could feel a churning in her stomach as everything started to make more sense: his late nights out, his constant need for money from her, and yes, his most recent move - the fancy dinner and late night romancing.

That bastard was playin' me all along, she thought to herself. Lisa's face turned red with anger, and she shot across into the bathroom with his phone in hand.

"Get out. Get the fuck out!" she exclaimed.

She took hold of the towel and threw it at Tony. He stood there naked and shocked by her sudden outburst. He begged her to tell him what was wrong, but the nauseous feeling in her stomach along with the blood rushing angrily through her body was more than she could handle. She could not take any more of his fake innocence.

"Look at your phone, you jerk!" she said, throwing the phone at him as well. When he picked up the phone, he realized that she had been reading his text messages; he tried to apologize and explain to her but she was not having any of it. With his towel around his waist and his body wet from his unfinished bath, she threw him out of her apartment.

The next couple of months were hard for Lisa, but during a conversation with one of her former co-workers, she was encouraged to date outside of her comfort zone.

"Look at me, I'm happily unemployed. I don't have to ever ask for anything twice, and he gives me everything I need. You really need to check out the website," the young lady, clothed in expensive apparel, told her.

As Lisa sat her computer, she was hesitant to visit the website her ex-co-worker had recommended. But the more she thought about it, the more curious she became. How exactly did this website work? She finally went to the link she had received and read through the first page and then clicked on the FAQ tab, browsing through it carefully. Call her old fashioned but she was never one to be looking for love online. It almost felt like high-end prostitution with a twist: rich, older men, looking for young attractive females to shower with money and other luxuries. They were just the type of men that she needed, considering the fact that she had been the one doing most of the giving in most of her relationships. These older men were called sugar daddies. As she sat there browsing through some of the profiles of the men on the website, she couldn't help but smile at the thought of getting a sugar daddy. She found one guy that did pique her interest. He had a mature yet very handsome look, he had a good profession and he did highlight the fact that he was looking for a young attractive woman to spoil. She quickly left him a brief message, stating that she was interested in getting to know him, and posted her email address and her telephone number so that he could contact her if he was interested.

The call came in late on Sunday afternoon about two weeks since she had sent him a message, on Sugardaddyforme.com. He had a firm, calm voice and he spoke perfect English. He introduced himself as James Warren, and invited her to dinner the following weekend, when he would be in Chicago. Lisa was so consumed with the sexiness in his voice that she happily agreed to their dinner date. Over the course of the week, he called her sometimes three times a day, and they spoke for hours on the phone, getting to know each other. He was the most romantic guy that she had ever spoken to. Maybe it was because of his age, but it was like a breath of fresh air speaking to him. Lisa found herself falling for this stranger that she had never met in person. They had had conversations where they could see each other over their webcams, and she was impressed so far by his attractive features, but she needed to see him to confirm everything.

The weekend came too soon; Lisa stood outside her apartment wearing one of her most expensive-looking outfits. It was a tight black dress that stopped a few inches above her knees and she paired it off with a pair of silver stilettos. As she waited for him, a luxurious-looking black Range Rover stopped a short distance ahead of her. She was not sure if it was her date, so she stood in the same spot and kept waiting for her date. The vehicle reversed, and the handsome man that she had been talking to online looked at her with his windows rolled all the way down. Before she could open the door, he stopped her. He got out and opened the door for her, but not before introducing himself. He was even more attractive in person. As they sat in the vehicle, her heart raced at the thought of this handsome man lying in her bed naked. No, it would never happen she thought to herself.

They had an amazing dinner, and their night was about to end when James walked her to her front door. She did not want this night to end; she leaned in and gently kissed his soft lips. Immediately, she felt the intense desire of his lips as he gave her a series of long, wet passionate kisses. She wanted more, she needed more. She quickly opened the door and led him inside where she found herself backed up against the wall while he devoured her with his hot wet tongue. Their pleasure was so intense that she almost melted in his arms.

He pulled back and whispered to her like the true gentleman he was, "If you want me to stop I will, but I do want you."

She pulled his lips back unto hers, a sign that let him know that she wanted to go all the way with him tonight. As they kissed, their hands explored each other's bodes. The attraction that Lisa felt for James was unlike anything that she had ever felt before. She had been caught off guard, expecting that he would have disappointed her when they met, but here she was, very impressed and wanting more. He gently released her lips, and they switched positions, his back was now on the wall. Lisa dropped down to her knees in front of him, as she unbuckled his belt as quickly as she could. His pants dropped to the floor leaving him with only his boxer shorts, which she also removed. His dick was beautiful; it was fully aroused, longer and thicker than any other dick she had ever seen. This must be what a mature dick looks like, she thought to herself as she took hold of his most beautiful asset and gently sucked on it. He groaned out loud, as he held her head unto his dick. She sucked his long hard dick, giving it gentle strokes with her tongue, and then increasing the momentum of her strokes. She sucked on his dick the way she sucked a sweet lollipop.

When she stopped for a minute, he extended his hand out and helped her to her feet only to pick her up in his arms, and seat her on her dinner table. He quickly removed her clothes and parted her legs while she lay on her back on the table. She shrieked when she felt his hot wet tongue swept inside her pussy. His tongue licked her pink pussy lips then slowly he moved his tongue upwards to her clitoris, where he lingered with slow gentle strokes.

"Oh, yeah, don't stop," she moaned as his tongue pleasured her unlike she had ever been pleasured in the past. Maybe his expert pussy-sucking skills came with experience over the years, she thought as she laid her head back trying to control herself. He continued to lick and suck her clit, and when that was not enough, he moved his tongue to her wet center, and proceeded to fuck her over and over with his hot tongue, wiggling it, inside her pussy hole. This was all too much for her to handle.

"Fuck me please, I wanna cum on your dick," she begged.

James pulled out his tongue from her wet pussy, and then penetrated her again with his dick. Now that she felt the full length of dick inside her, she longed to feel the tenderness of his tongue once more. His thrusts were long, and hard, and he looked down directly into her eyes with every thrust. She was enjoying herself, licking her lips and moaning out profanities as she received the best fuck of her life. She was in sweet surrender when suddenly his momentum changed and he was now thrusting his dick inside her pussy violently. It was no longer a thrust; it was more of a slam. In and out, he slammed his huge cock in her wet pussy causing her to scream out in pain-filled ecstasy. Finally, when he was about to climax, he pulled out his dick from her pussy and exploded, shooting out his hot cum all over her belly. She too let out a loud shriek as she reached her climax together with him.

They both looked at each other in amazement, both of them surprised at what had just happened. They sat on the couch and talked for about two hours straight, drinking a bottle of red wine that she had been saving up for a special occasion. Finally, he got up and was about to leave. Lisa found herself wanting more of him, and it was terribly hard to see him leave. As she walked him to the door, she made a U-turn and held on to his hand, inviting him to follow her upstairs to her room. There was no hesitation on his part, as he followed this attractive young woman. When they got to the room, Lisa had him lay down on her bed, and then stripped him naked once more. His dick had been asleep, but the feel of her wet tongue on it was gradually bringing it back to life.

She sucked his dick long and hard while gently caressing his tender balls. He was groaning out in pleasure, and she was surprised when he pulled his dick out of her mouth only to pull her upwards unto it. He held her up, and carefully helped her pussy find its way on his dick. He made several noises from the pleasure of having her riding his dick. Lisa rocked her pussy back and forth on his long cock, her breasts bouncing up and down as she lost herself in the moment. He held firmly onto her ass, keeping her secure as she rode his cock. It was the best experience of her life; he was a sugar daddy in every way. They came together, their moans echoing loudly. Later, the two of them tried to calm down and figure what the next step in their sugar daddy-sugar daughter relationship might be. Lisa did know that her days of being with young broke guys were over; she was not going to waste her time with trash when she had pure gold right there.

James ordered breakfast in bed for the two of them and expressed his desire to continue seeing Lisa. She happily accepted him, and when he was leaving, he reached out into his briefcase and pulled out a small black box. "This is for you, I had a lovely time," he said as he presented her with this gift. Lisa was surprised; she had not been expecting anything from him. Little did she know, this was just the first of many gifts that he would shower her with.

SHALA BREECE

4 HER LOVE SPELL

This was it, her moment of truth. If she was going to regret this, now would be the perfect time to back out. She held on to her VISA debit card contemplating whether she was making the right decision. There were several great testimonials on the website, and their service fees were quite reasonable in comparison to their other online competitors. Sarah took a deep breath and finally decided to move forward with her plans. She browsed through the list of love spells one last time and then checked the tiny box next to the third one among a long list of about ten.

Simply Irresistible – Attract a new lover or reunite with an old lover with this powerful love-binding spell.

There was a simple form that she had to fill out with her name, details of her situation, and desired outcome. After completing the form, her payment went through and she received a confirmation email stating that the payment had been received and her spell would be cast by Master Psychic Doreen within the next hour.

The uncertain look that she had on her face faded away as a wicked smile formed in the corners of her bright red lips. The thought of Brandon, weak and unable to resist her, made her feel like she had just made a wise investment in her future. Now that she had paid for this love spell, all that was left for her to do is wait. There were a few sentences in the website's FAQ section that mentioned that after spells could take a few hours or in more serious cases, they could take about two weeks after they're cast to come into fruition. So all she had to do now was wait.

Sarah Hunter was an attractive woman of color; she had her dream job, her dream car, and her dream house, but the only thing missing was Brandon. A gorgeously handsome African American man named Brandon Harris had captured Sarah's attention from the time she was in high school. Although he was slightly older than her, Brandon seemed to have everything that she wanted in a man. She finally exchanged telephone numbers with him a few months ago after running into each other at a club. After that night, she had tried to call him on the number, but she was never able to get him; it always went straight to his voicemail.

It was about ten in the night when her phone rang. Sarah rolled over on her huge lonesome bed, and stretched out her hand to get her cell phone that had been on her nightstand. "Hey Sarah," a masculine voice that had a little bit of familiarity said. Sarah pondered for a bit, trying to figure out who was this mysterious man. Her thoughts were interrupted when he reintroduced himself. It was Brandon. He said that he had been thinking about her the entire day, and he had felt like he needed to speak to her. Sarah smiled upon hearing his confession; in her heart, she knew that her spell had started working. "You can come over to my place if you want," she told him, secretly hoping that he would come over. Her invitation was accepted and after giving him the direction to her house, she heard his knocks at the door about half an hour later.

Sarah was so confident in the power of her love spell that she opened the door wearing nothing but a white bathrobe. As Brandon strode past her, she carefully examined every inch of his handsome body with desire fill eyes. Although he was dressed in simple attire, his blue jeans and white t-shirt complimented his physique perfectly. She walked up to a small wine cabinet in her kitchen and pulled out a bottle of wine she had been saving. As they sipped on the red wine, Sarah moved in closer to him, so close that she could feel his smooth dark chocolate skin against her caramel-toned skin. She leaned in towards him and her mouth quickly found his, as their tongues danced together in sweet ecstasy. His hands slowly made their way between the robe she covered her naked flesh with, and cupped one of her firmly rounded breasts. They broke off from their passionate kiss and his lips made their way down to her perched nipples, sucking them one by one. She moaned out from the pleasure of his tongue on her skin.

When she had enough, she got up and stripped off her robe completely. His eyes lit up when she saw her completely naked moving her hips seductively. Soon after he stood up to join her and they shared another long passionate kiss; however this time Sarah slowly undressed him. Satisfied that they were both naked, she gave him a gentle push that caused him to fall back unto the couch; she went down on her knees in front the couch and parted his legs. His dick was long and black, and she could not ward off her desire to suck it. So she gently stroked his length with her hot wet tongue. He cleared his throat, as he pushed back a little and made a low groan. Sarah enjoyed seeing how uneasy he was and increased the strength of her suction on his manhood. Her strokes changed from long, slow strokes to harder full-blown sucks. She flicked her tongue back and forth on the purplish head of the dick, while her hands caressed his balls. She could tell that he was enjoying the experience because he could hardly seat still.

Sarah realized that sucking his dick was sending sensations throughout her body. Just the way he twisted and turned his body to the touch of her tongue had her juices trickling down like a fountain. Her pussy ached for the feel of his dick inside her, and so she finally released his dick from her mouth and mounted it instead with her pussy. "O God, yeah!" escaped his lips as her wet cunt rocked back and forth on his dick. She could feel her insides stretched to its maximum as she rode his dick. He seemed to have been enjoying it because he was actively involved in caressing her nipples with his tongue as she bounced up and down on his dick. The more she rode his dick, the closer she got to her orgasm. Finally, just as she was about to climax, she felt him hold on to her hip and gave her few hard upward thrusts before his hot cum exploded inside her pussy.

They sat back on the couch and held each other for almost the entire night before moving to her bedroom.

The following morning, Sarah was awakened by a strange feeling that ran from the tip of her big toe and sent shock waves through her body. She thought she was having a good dream, but reality soon hit her when she felt the sensation narrow in directly between her legs. She opened her eyes and was shocked to see Brandon's head between her legs. The sensations she had been feeling were the result of him sucking her big toe and working his way up to sucking her pussy. His tongue had gripped firmly onto her clitoris while his fingers explored the insides of her cunt. Using his fingers, he gently parted her pussy lips and stroked it from the bottom up. Each time he got to the top, he gave her clit a long hard suck, gently tugging with his teeth before releasing it. She moaned out with every long stroke that he gave her, and fingers dug into the sheets as she tried desperately to control herself. He stopped for a brief moment and lifted his head up from where it had securely position between her legs. "You like this don't you?" he asked as he now used his fingers to stroke her moist flesh.

Sarah's eyes had been closed as she enjoyed the sweet sensations that he had been bringing about with his tongue. She was so engulfed in it all that she did not even hear his question. Again, he asked but this time, when he asked he used two of his fingers and penetrated her insides. He had definitely captured her attention now. "Please, don't stop, lick my pussy, I like that" she said with desperation in her voice. She needed to feel him devouring her insides with his tongue; it had felt like heaven. He seemed to be an expert at eating pussy, and she was impressed. He obliged to her request and buried his tongue deep down inside her pussy. This time, he licked and sucked her cunt like never before. She moaned and moaned as her fingers ran through his full head of hair. He ate her pussy like a lion devouring its prey, and he would occasionally pull away and just look at her swollen pussy with a look of admiration on his face.

"I want your cum on my tongue Sarah, I want all of you"

Tiny spasms ran through her body, as he used his wicked tongue to fuck her pussy. Deeper and deeper he plunged his tongue inside her, flicking it back and forth as his hands made their way up to her nipples. She was receiving double the pleasure, and finally her body gave in to the intense pressure. She gave a loud moan, "Oh fuck, yeah! I'm cumming." Her body jolted violently against his tongue, as her legs twisted and stretched as if she had been tied down and was trying to get released. He licked and sucked her juices that she had just released and made a pleasing sound that let her know that he had enjoyed eating her pussy out. She closed her eyes and took in several deep breaths as she tried to calm down.

Suddenly, Sarah felt a mass of pressure penetrating her insides; she quickly opened her eyes. Brandon had now mounted her and had his huge dick thrusting up against her moistness. She moaned out to him and eased off on the pressure by pulling out a little. He planted a series of soft kisses on her lips and then proceeded to continue his thrusts. His hard dick made her body quiver as it made its way deeper and deeper inside her. When his full length had filled her pussy hole, he pulled out again and gave her a single hard thrust without the gentleness of the one before. She closed her eyes, as he gave her a series of long, gentle strokes, mixed with some harder quicker strokes. The bed rocked from side to side, up and down, as the two of them fucked like animals on it. The sounds of her moaning and his panting heightened their arousal and made the fucking more pleasurable.

He stopped and pulled out after a while, instructing her to get on her hands and knees as her prepared to fuck her in her ass.

Although Sarah had had anal sex before, she knew it was quite painful and she was a bit hesitant about his new position. Before allowing him to thrust his dick up her ass, she stretched out her hands and reached over to the top draw of her nightstand, pulling out a tube of lube. She gave it to him and he proceeded to rub the hot liquid all over her anus. When he was satisfied with the amount of lubrication he had applied, he tossed the tub to the side of the bed and held onto her ass firmly as he slowly penetrated her asshole. Her body tensed and repelled his dick for a minute, but he was determined to fuck her in her anus, and so he kept pushing his dick inside her.

"Oh fuck that hurts!" she shrieked as his dick finally made its way inside her. He leaned in and gave her a soft kiss in the center of her back. He took his time with her and somehow managed to get his hands around her hip area, and he was now rubbing onto her clitoris and pleasuring her. His fingers flicked back and forth on her clitoris, giving it small circular motions and rubbing hard against it sometimes. Suddenly, all the pain that she was feeling from his dick inside her forbidden hole, as she would refer to it, was slowly disappearing. A pleasurable, sensational feeling she had never experienced replaced the pain and she found herself, jerking backwards unto his dick. This was exactly the encouragement that he needed. He gripped onto her ass and gave her several long hard thrusts, and each one sent ripples through her asshole. He seemed to be enjoying this even more than he had been enjoying fucking her pussy. He began smacking her ass with his thrusts, and he soon added a few profanities every time he smacked her ass.

Finally, with a loud groan and a hard thrust, he exploded inside her. He grabbed onto her ass, as if he wanted to ensure that all his cum had securely made it into her asshole. They both collapsed on the bed soon after, too tired and exhausted to even get dressed.

The following morning they said their goodbyes as he left and she got ready for work. The first thing she did when she got to work was go to the website to write her testimonial. Before she could click on the little publish button at the bottom of the page, a thought crossed her mind. What if this wsd a one-time thing? What if he never comes back to her? Just the thought made her too sad to even continue her post. She decided to wait a few weeks before posting anything on the website. She slouched back in her huge leather chair and closed her eyes as flashes of her erotic experience with Brandon consumed her thoughts.

As her day went by, she found that it was harder and harder to focus on her work. She kept daydreaming about Brandon, and she felt the urge to call him or drop by his office. Finally, when she realized that she could not do any work, she decided to call him for directions to his office. He was a small time lawyer, and he had a small office in the middle of the town; it would only take her about ten minutes to get there. With her car keys in hand, she left her office and drove over to his office.

His office was empty, like a ghost town. "Where's everyone?" she asked him curiously.

"It's just me and my secretary, Molly, who's out sick today," he replied as he made his way over to where she was standing.

He stretched his hand past her and locked the door that she had just come in. Now the two of them were completely alone and undisturbed. His lips felt like pure heaven, as he swept her away in a passionate kiss. Their mouths lingered together, as their tongues engaged in a tug of passionate war. He moved up against her, and soon her back was up against the wall in his office. Soon enough, his hand made their way up her tight black pencil skirt, pulling her panties aside; he stroked her insides of her tights. Her pussy was already wet from the intensity of their kiss, and he pulled back looking at her in amazement. He looked at his two middle fingers that were drenched in her wetness and proceeded to place it next to her mouth.

"I want you to taste your sweetness," he said as he requested her to lick his wet fingers. Without hesitation, she took hold of his fingers and sucked off her juices.

"Delicious," she said licking her lips and giving him a wicked little smile.

This made him all the hornier for her. He pressed up against her even closer now, and they shared another deep passionate kiss. This time their desire for each other had intensified, and they practically ripped off each other's clothes. She was wearing a pink lace thong with a matching bra, and he took a step back just to admire her sexy body. "You must have planned to drop by," he said, as he popped the bra open from the front where it hooked.

Sarah had been in such a good mood in the morning that she had pulled out this Victoria Secret lingerie set that she had been saving up for a special occasion. She had not had any plans of going to visit him at the time; she had just worn it, just because. Her breasts had popped out when he had unhooked the bra, and he now had one of her nipples in his mouth sucking vivaciously. She had never had office sex before, but if this was how it felt, then she was definitely going to be having more of it. As he pleasured her with his tongue, her juices trickled down her pussy, saturating her panties to the point where she desperately longed to have them ripped off her flesh. It seemed like he read her mind because while he had her nipples in his mouth, his hands worked their way between her thighs, and with one hard pull, he ripped off the flimsy thong that she had been wearing. A moan of pleasure escaped her desire filled lips, and he stroked her flesh with his fingers some more.

"You gonna make me fuck you on this wall, Sarah," Brandon groaned as the desire to be inside Sarah got more and more intense. He finally whipped out his erect dick; without hesitation, he lifted one of her legs up, allowing him better access to her pussy. The feel of his huge dick had her squirming up against the wall. Her pussy was tender and swollen from the pounding it had received earlier on during the day, at her house. Almost every thrust had her moaning in sweet pain. Her huge breasts bounced up and down, as he slammed his dick inside her. She found herself moaning out profanities to him and begging him to go easy on her. However, Brandon was lost in the moment and ignored her moans; he continued fucking her hard.

Sarah was caught off guard when he suddenly flung her upwards and held her securely upwards against his body, as he thrust his dick inside her wet pussy. This move shocked her and impressed her at the same time. Her body reacted positively to his position, and her juices ran all the way down his dick and almost to his balls. He held onto her tightly in the air, as he continued to give her several hard thrusts. He stopped for a brief moment, still holding her upwards and finally propped her over his desk. Her ass was popped out facing him, allowing him rear entry. He must really like fucking her in her ass, she thought to herself as she braced herself for the pain of anal sex. She was shocked when he ignored her anus and made his way downwards to the small entrance of her pussy. As his dick found her pussy hole, he groaned and grabbed onto her ass and proceed to fuck her doggy style. It was amazing; he was using his fingers to stimulate her clitoris, while his dick gently stroked her insides from the back.

Soon he increased the momentum of his thrusts, and she jerked out a little when she felt his firm grip on a handful of her hear. She felt like a pornstar, and she cried out for more. He continued to increase the speed and force of his thrust while holding onto her hair. "Yeah, baby, fuck me, just like that, ooohhh, yeah. Fuck!" she moaned as he pounded her insides over and over with his cock. He too was groaning and complimenting her on how tight and sweet her pussy was. Sarah could feel her juices trickling down, and she finally closed her eyes and had her release. Her release set him off and his thrusts became even more vicious than before; she could tell that he was about to cum. He gave her several hard smacks across her ass as he gave her some quick hard thrusts. "OH, Yeah. Shit! God damn girl, fuck!" he groaned loudly as he exploded as sea of hot cum into her pussy.

They took about ten minutes just to calm down from their moment of ecstasy. Her cunt was dripping with cum, as she hurriedly made her way to the bathroom to try to clean up and return to her office before her boss noticed she was gone.

When she made it back to the office, Sarah felt a little confused; she did not quite understand why she had so desperately needed to see Brandon. After all, he was the one that she put the charm on.

A scary thought crossed her mind, but she tried to brush it off. It can't be, she thought as she pulled up the website where she had purchased the spell from the beginning. As she read through the FAQ's once more, her fears were confirmed. Right in front of her in fine print:

All love spells are binding. Your lover will be hopelessly attracted to you, and likewise you will be hopelessly attracted to your lover. The feeling and strong desire to be with each other will be implanted in both of you.

In her efforts to be with the love of her life, she had not only cast a love spell on him, she had also cast a love spell on herself. She found Brandon simply irresistible, and she needed to see him again tonight.

5 GOOD COP, NAUGHTY SLUT

Nancy Patton made her way to the bar for one last drink that the bartender was hesitant to give to her. Although he was appreciative of the tons of money she was spending, everyone in Ruston knew who her father was. Jeff Patton was Ruston's best prosecutor; he had never lost a case, but during recent times, he had become known for his no-nonsense attitude toward his daughter. Nancy Patton tried everything she could to be her own person and move out of her father's shadows, but, just like a shadow, he was everywhere she went.

People were even afraid to associate with her for fear of getting into trouble with her father. Tonight had been no different; the bartender did not even want to serve her too many drinks because he feared that he would be on the receiving end of her father's fury if anything were to happen to her.

She had just about had it with everyone treating her like a leper. She got up on one of the tables and began stripping as if it was a stage at a gentleman's club. The majority of the people at the bar were men, and they went wild as she seductively moved her hips from side to side, slipping out of her blouse first and then her pants. She held her clothes up in the air for a moment before spinning them around in her hands and then tossing them into the small audience of men.

"We want to see titties!" one man shouted as another brave man walked up to where she was and gently stroked her long legs. Still on the table, she went down on her knees and was now caressing her full breasts, which had begun to pop out of her bra.

Officer Robert Givens walked into the bar, his eyes scanning the entire environs as he tried to locate the cause of the racket. It had been a slow night for him, and he had been relaxing in his car enjoying some music when he got the call from dispatch. There had been some disturbances at a local club, and since he was really close to the scene, it was his duty to go over there. Now that he was here, he did not really see a disturbance, but he walked up to the bartender that had made the distress call to find out what exactly was the problem.

"She's out of control officer, and her dad will probably have this place shut down if he finds out she's here stripping on tables and stuff," he said frantically.

Robert made his way through the center of the crowd to see who this young woman was.

His jaw dropped as his eyes locked gazes with Jeff Patton's daughter, Nancy. He and Nancy had gone to college together, and at one point, he had a huge crush on her. However, he had never gotten to express his feelings for her because of the way he had seen her father scare away the guys who tried to date her. There had even been this one guy that had ended up locked away in jail for a few days, when Jeff pulled up all the traffic tickets that he had not been paying.

"Nancy, get off that table right now," he said with his arm stretched out to help her get down.

She looked a little shocked and embarrassed to see him; grabbing hold of his hand, she made her way off the table. He should have arrested her for indecent exposure but he could not; she was a girl that he thought was the most beautiful girl in the world. He led her to his car and opened the back door, allowing her to get in.

In the car, Nancy begged and pleaded with him to not take her to the station. "Just drop me off at home; I'll just go to bed, I promise. My dad will kill me if I get charged," she pleaded with him.

She did not know that he had no intentions of taking her to the station; he was going to take her to her apartment and see her get in safely. As he stopped in front of her apartment, she stopped begging. He got out of the car and walked her to her front door. She asked him to come in, saying that she just wanted to talk. At first, he did not believe her because in her state of mind, he doubted that she would be able to have an intellectual conversation, but she was a coy little temptress and he finally gave in.

Her apartment was just as beautiful as he had always imagined that it would be. His police instincts had kicked in as his eyes carefully perused the place. She had gone to the kitchen to get him some tea, while he sat on the couch waiting. He heard her call out to him, asking him to come over to the kitchen. He got up and walked into the kitchen, but he could not see her.

"Where'd you go!" he called, before his attention was captured by a voice from behind the kitchen counter.

Like a goddess, she slowly rose from behind the counter. She was completely naked holding a brown bottle in hand and plump red cherry between her teeth. Robert looked at her with complete amazement; he realized that the bottle contained chocolate syrup, a fact that made him unable to move as she moved swiftly toward him.

Nancy had a beautiful caramel complexion, being of African descent. Her breasts were like two huge melons adorned with temptingly attractive brown nipples. She had a slender body and beautiful thick black hair that hung down to her shoulders. His dick throbbed; he had gotten an arousal from the time he saw her on the table almost naked at the bar. Her lips made contact with his, and although he wanted to resist her, he couldn't. It was like a dream come true. Her tongue explored the insides of his mouth causing tiny spasms to run through his body. He wanted her so badly, but everything in him kept telling him that what they were doing was wrong. He finally broke away from her heated kiss, and taking a deep breath, he said he had to leave.

Robert felt her soft touch on his hand as he tried to leave. "Don't go, stay with me tonight," she said with a look of desire and desperation in her eyes.

He did not even have time to get an answer out before she was back directly in front of him with an intense look in her eyes. She stroked the crotch of his pants as her tongue caressed the nape of his neck. He felt like he would melt under the pressure of her touch. When she released his tongue, she slowly went down on her knees and unzipped his pants. Her hands made it into his underwear and whipped out his dick.

Her tongue was wet and hot, and he groaned with pleasure as she took him in and an out of her mouth, sucking his full length. Suddenly, there was another feeling on his dick; his eyes that had been closed were now opened as he looked down to see what was happening. Nancy had drizzled some chocolate syrup along his dick. Soon her tongue was back on his dick, this time licking off the chocolate syrup. The contrast of the chocolate syrup on his pale cream toned dick made the experience all the more erotic to him. He watched as she licked his dick inch by inch making sounds of pleasure as if she were enjoying a delicious dessert. The more she sucked, the harder his dick became, and it got to a point where his knees felt weak from all the sensations she brought about with her tongue.

She must have seen his knees shaking because she stopped her blowjob for a minute and walked over to the dining room. She returned to the kitchen, dragging a chair behind her. She placed the chair in the middle of the kitchen where she had been and instructed Robert to have a seat on it. She got down on her knees and parted his legs, and her tongue made its way back to his cock. She drizzled some more chocolate syrup and used her tongue to suck it all off once more. She gave his dick long strokes and then shorter strokes toward the head of his dick, flicking her tongue around its round, pinkish head occasionally. As she sucked his dick, she used her hand to gently cup his balls and caressed them. Robert thought he would lose his mind; he could feel his blood rushing down to his dick, and he knew that he might explode in her mouth at any time.

He did not want this to be all about him, and he felt the urge to pleasure her as well. He wanted to taste the insides of her pussy, to lick it, to suck it, and even to drizzle it with some chocolate syrup. It took all his strength to pull her lips away from his dick, as he got down on floor, inviting her to join him. To his surprise, she joined him, but not exactly in the position he had thought she would; in something better. She leaned over him, with her pussy propped up against his mouth, while his dick was directly in front of her mouth. She gripped onto his dick with her mouth, while he in turn took hold of her clit with his mouth. Her pussy was dripping wet, and every now and then she would release his dick from her mouth and let out soft moans while his tongue stroked her insides. He reached over to where she had the chocolate syrup, poured syrup on his fingers, and pasted it along the insides of her flesh. Then using his tongue, he licked every bit of the syrup that was in her sweet pussy.

Robert could feel her body quivering as he sucked her pussy, and he also felt her grip on his dick tighten as she now moved her mouth viciously from the top of his dick to the bottom. He in turn increased the intensity of his sucks while gently pulling onto her clitoris before giving it a few flicks with his tongue. Suddenly, she released his dick and pulled against his tongue; she got up and walked over to the back of the counter. Being on the floor, he could not see what she was doing, but seconds later, she returned with a block of ice in her hand. He was amazed at how creative she was because he had always imagined that she would be more of the reserved type when in the sack. She placed the ice in her mouth and then placed her coldness on his hard dick. He groaned out loud; the feel of the ice on his dick brought about mixed feelings as it literally sent shivers through his body. With the ice and his dick in her mouth, she managed to wiggle the ice around his dick. It brought about a new sensation for him, and he gripped onto her clitoris, sucking it long and hard. She finally pulled her icy mouth away from his dick and covered the entire dick with chocolate syrup. Her lips soon followed, slowly stroking his cock as she licked off all the chocolate syrup. He was now nibbling on her clitoris, and her pussy was jolting so hard against his mouth that he had to use his hand to keep her in position. He wanted her to feel an equal amount of pleasure. As he sucked her pussy, she sucked his dick, and they both shivered in pure ecstasy as they neared a thunderous climax.

His dick thrust upward into her mouth almost touching the back of her throat, and he exploded his semen inside her wanting mouth. Her pussy was also moving back and forth, as she finally reached her climax with his last long lingering stroke on her wet flesh. It took them a while to calm down, as they remained in position. She finally got up and as he lay on the floor, he could see her legs shaking as if she had not fully recovered from her orgasm. She stretched out her hands to him and helped him up. She offered him a drink, now that they had finished fucking.

Why not, he thought. His night had been wild enough, maybe a drink would help him relax and put things into perspective. They made their way to the couch as they took shots of vodka. The more they had to drink, the more relaxed they became, and soon a horny feeling crept up upon him once more. He looked at his watch. To his surprise, it was well over two hours since they had enjoyed each other on the floor of her kitchen. How quickly time had passed.

Robert could feel his dick throbbing more intensely than before, thanks to the alcohol in his system.

"This must have been how she was feeling earlier on during the night," he thought.

He tried to control this unbearable desire to fuck her. He looked into her desire filled eyes; they said everything he wanted to know. They were both still naked, and it was easy for her to begin to stroke his dick with her hands. The more she stroked, the harder and longer the dick became. Soon it had reached its full length, and he was longing to feel her insides of her pussy on it. It was as if she could read his thoughts because she suddenly got up from his side and mounted his dick. She rocked her body back and forth as her pussy slowly begun wetting his cock with her sweet juices. She locked lips with him, as she rode his dick; her tongue explored the insides of his mouth as her breasts bounced up and down.

He had always been attracted to breasts, and so he could not just sit back while her breasts bounced happily in front of him. He pulled away from her kiss and grabbed hold of her breasts, placing one in his mouth while his fingers caressed the nipples of her other breasts. She moaned out loud, as he flicked his tongue around the nipple.

"Oh yeah, suck those fucking tits," she moaned as she jerked back and forth on his dick.

He could feel her pussy contracting from the pleasure of his dick inside it. He gripped firmly unto her hips and pulled her body hard against his. She gave a loud shriek as he took control of the situation penetrating her insides with the full length of his long dick.

"Oh fuck yeah, you like fucking this little slut don't you?" she asked as she ground up against his dick with her pussy.

She had just referred to herself as a slut. He had never seen her as a slut, but she seemed to be enjoying referring to herself as a slut. Robert was so impressed with her dick riding skills that he could hardly control himself. He felt like his climax was near. How could such an innocent sweet looking girl turn out to be such a naughty slut? If her dad only knew all the things that she had done to him tonight.

Again, she asked him another question that took him off guard. "You like fucking my little cunt don't you? You want to tear it up don't you?" she asked in a horse low-toned voice.

He responded by nodding his head and thrusting upward inside her with more force. She ran her fingers through her hair. Finally, he had had enough, he wanted to show her the full extent of his dick. He was somewhat tired of her dirty talk, and he wanted to see her melt under the pressure of his dick. He pulled her up off his dick and bent her over the armrest of the couch with her ass popped out toward him.

"Oh God, fuck, shit!" she shrieked as he viciously thrust his hard dick inside her pussy from the back.

Gripping her ass, he shoved his dick inside her over and over; each thrust was harder than the one before. The air was filled with her cries as her fingers dug into the cushion for support. Her pussy was the best he had had in a long while. He gave her a soft smack on the ass, a punishment for all the naughty things she had been doing that night. It did not surprise him when she asked him to smack her ass again. He happily obliged, this time giving her a harder smack than what he had previously given her. Robert could see tiny ripples running through her thick ass cheeks. She was definitely well endowed in the butt area, and her voluptuous ass made fucking her from the back all the more enjoyable. Her ass bounced back and forth like a vibrator on his dick. Using his hand, he parted her ass chicks and penetrated her insides even deeper. She jerked forward from the intensity of his full length inside her.

Robert continued to give her a series of long hard thrusts followed by shorter harder thrusts. Finally, he could no longer control himself; he launched inside her with full force. She moaned and cried once she even begged him to stop. But he did not stop; she deserved it as she had been a naughty little slut, and so she would receive punishment.

The more he fucked her, the closer he came to the brink of his climax. Suddenly, her cries changed and they were now loud moans of pleasure, asking him to fuck her harder. He fucked her harder while she begged, and her body quivered as she let out a loud shriek as she came all over his hard dick. When he saw that she had climaxed, he released and there was an explosion of his hot liquid inside her pussy. His dick lingered in her pussy for a while until he was fully satisfied that he had stuffed the inside of her pussy with every drop of his come.

He pulled back, parted her ass cheeks, and peeked in to see his cum dripping down her pussy. Her pussy squirted out their cum like a waterfall, and he could not resist thrusting his finger inside her one last time. As he pulled out his wet finger, he brought it up to her mouth,

"Here's a taste of your pussy and my cum," he said as he put the finger closer to her lips, awaiting her to suck his finger. She was more than happy to taste the mixture of their juices, licking her lips when she was done sucking his long finger. They sat back on the couch for a minute to calm down, and then he finally left. He feared that if he had stayed any longer, they would probably end up fucking again. As he went into his car, he felt exhausted and used; he had never expected all of what had just happened to go down. He drove away as images of her naked body kept replaying in his mind.

Robert had just taken his shower after a long day at work. He was seated on his couch watching TV when he heard the knock on his front door. He had not been expecting anyone

tonight so he hesitantly went to answer the door. "Who could it be?" he thought to himself as he turned the doorknob.

She was dressed in black cloak, and from the looks of it did not seem like she was wearing anything under it. Her beautiful hair glistened in the moonlight, and her bright red lips let him know that she was here with one thing on her mind.

"Can I come in?" she asked with a wicked little smile on her face.

A few seconds passed before he slowly stepped aside to allow her entry to his home. She strode across his living and made her way to his couch while he looked on with gluttonous eyes. As she sat on the couch, she raised one leg up on the couch, while the other remained on the floor. She unfastened her cloak and exposed the mound of her pussy. His eyes opened wider in amazement as he instantly became aroused. He looked on as she used her fingers to stroke her pussy, pulling it up to her lips and sucking her juices. "Did she drive over here with a wet pussy?" he wondered as he moved in closer to her.

He could hardly believe his eyes; he had been at home, relaxing, and she had found him. "How did you know where I live?" he asked her curiously.

"A good cop is easy to find," she replied, as she got up slowly and made her way to him. When they met, her lips devoured him in a passionate kiss, and she began undressing him, right there in the middle of his living room.

That night they fucked for what seemed like hours with every stroke and every position being different from the last. The entire time she amazed him with her techniques and even with the way she spoke to him. Yes, she was definitely a naughty little slut.

6 EROTIC ADVENTURES OF THE TEAM

The crowd roared as Mason scored the amazing touchdown which secured their win. This was his third football game and the first win for his team this season. As they left the field and made their way to the locker room, the frenzy of the crowd followed them. Before the game, it seemed like bad luck had been following the team; they had lost almost every game last season, and this season had not looked too good for them either.

It seemed like everyone had lost hope in them and it felt good to feel the support of their fans once more. Mason remembered the conversation that he had with one of the cheerleaders before the game. Jenna had been pessimistic and even gone so far as to say, "It will take a miracle for you guys to win. In fact, if you guys win, I promise I'll suck all your dicks."

Thinking back, Mason could see the arrogance on her face when she had made her bold statement. She had been so confident that they would lose this game. A wicked smile formed on the corner of his lips as he envisioned what it might feel like having Jenna on her knees while her mouth was stuffed with several huge cocks. He thought that the after party that they had planned would definitely be interesting if Jenna would have to make good on her promise sometime during that event.

The hours before the party seemed to fly by as Mason got dressed and made his way to Nathan's house. Nathan, their quarterback, was one of the more privileged guys on the team. His parents owned several huge houses, and they had been generous enough to give Nathan his own house when he turned twenty-one. The house was in a secluded area, about ten minutes off the main road, and it included amenities such as a huge pool, gym, and a full bar, which made it seem like a hotel. As Mason opened the door, he was greeted by a crowd of loud rowdy students and booming music. He forced his way through the tight crowd and finally found the kitchen area where most of his team members stood around drinking and chatting. One of the guys from the team who had not been in the kitchen came calling out to them. He wanted them to follow him upstairs.

The six guys quickly followed him up the stairs, where he led them into the last bedroom on the left. Mason could hardly believe his eyes, and he swallowed hard when he saw the surprise that had been awaiting them in the room. In fact, it was not just a surprise; it was three surprises. There were three half-naked girls on the bed fondling and playing with each other's breasts.

"Hey girls, the guys are here," Neil said as he strode across the room and went over to the bed. The girls welcomed him with open arms, and when he lay down on the center of the bed, they stroked his body with their fingers and their tongues. The other guys smiled, realizing it was going to be a wild night.

One of the girls was Jenna, the cheerleader with the big mouth. She had her hair all curled up and looked different. Normally, she would have her hair pulled back in a ponytail. He had to admit that she looked beautiful and he longed to feel her lips and her pussy on his dick. He and Nathan focused their attention on Jenna while Caleb and Patrick went over to one of her friends. The last girl was paired up with Neil and Keith. Now that they had picked which of the three girls they wanted, each pair of the friends began their individual ménage-a-trios. The room was filled with soft giggles from the six girls who were obviously enjoying the experience.

As he looked on, Mason could see Caleb on the floor with one of the girls bent over him, sucking his dick while Patrick was fucking her from the back. The girl looked like one of the girls in the porn videos that he had been watching. She had a beautiful tanned complexion and silky black hair. He could see ripples running through her ass cheeks as Patrick slammed his dick inside her. She must have been enjoying it, because her body moved in perfect timing with his. Patrick was definitely enjoying it; he was talking dirty loud enough for Mason to hear every word. He was also using his large masculine hands to deliver powerful smacks on her tiny ass. Mason's attention was soon captured away by sweet moaning sounds; he looked over to the bed where Neil had been with Keith. The two guys had positioned themselves in a way that each of them was able to fuck her at the same time, one in her ass and the other in pussy. Mason peeked a little and saw the narrow gap between the two dicks; they had somehow managed to pull this off, and everyone was getting maximum pleasure.

"You just gonna stand there?" a soft familiar female voice said.

Mason turned to his side to see Nathan laying down flat on his back on the carpeted floor. Jenna had already mounted him and was riding his dick. They seemed to be so entwined that he did not quite see where he would fit in. As he made his way to them, they stopped and adjusted their positioning a little. He was now able to get his dick inside her with their change in position. He got down on his knees while Jenna had her pussy positioned on Nathan's dick and parted her ass cheeks.

He could see her anus; it was beautiful and inviting. He whipped out his dick from his boxer shorts and stroked it a few times, lubricating it with his saliva. Now, he was ready. Giving her anus a swab of his saliva to serve as her lubrication, he gently tried to penetrate her back door entry. Her body tensed up, and Nathan could feel it, the muscles of her anus were so tight that it seemed impossible to get his long dick in there.

"Easy, Mason" Nathan said jokingly. "You don't want to give her a heart attack."

Once more, he tried to penetrate her anus with his dick, but it still would not go inside. This time, he decided to do something to help her relax. Bending over, Mason used his hot tongue to caress her anus. His tongue stroked and traced the small hole causing her to moan out in pleasure. He increased her pleasure by penetrating her anus with his tongue. His tongue ravished her anus, and soon, she began begging him to fuck her from behind.

She did not have to ask him a second time; he quickly pulled his tongue away from the hole and again lubricated his dick with his saliva. He also put some on his index finger and brought it down to her ass whole swabbing the area with his natural lubrication one more time. His dick was hard, harder than it had ever been, thanks to the sight of the other women fucked by two men; that alone could have guaranteed him a good cum. He stroked his dick a few times before launching the attack on her anus. This time, her flesh was more welcoming; as he penetrated her, she cringed a little, but Nathan helped by capturing her lips with his in a hot passionate kisses. His dick slowly expanded the walls of her anus, and finally he was able to get his full length inside her. It was like nothing he had ever felt before; her hole was so tight; he was sure it was her first time having anal sex. He gently began to thrust his dick inside her, his hand caressing her ass at the same time.

He could feel the ecstasy building up inside, and as he fucked her, Nathan matched his strokes in perfect time. In and out, his dick went inside her ass whole while Nathan laid in the bottom, fucking her in a supportive rhythm. She moaned and asked them to fuck her harder.

"You want this shit harder?" he groaned as he realized that he was being gentle with her while she wanted hard rough sex. Mason increased the momentum of his thrust, and her body jerked back and forth while she moaned out in pleasure. It was like sweet heaven in the room for Mason because as he fucked her, he could see his other team members fucking the other girls, and he could hear them moaning out in ecstasy as well.

Mason realized that most of the other guys had changed positions. Neil and Keith, who had been fucking their girl at the same time, had now switched over to where the girl was riding Neil's dick while Keith's cock was stuffed in her mouth. It looked like fun over there, but he doubted that it was better than the feeling he was getting from fucking Jenna's tight little asshole.

"Oh God Jenna, I'm Gonna cum," Mason heard Nathan groan as he gave her several hard upwards thrusts with his dick.

Her body bounced against his as the impact of Nathan's body on her was too great. Finally, with a loud groan, Nathan released and shot his liquid inside her pussy. Nathan slipped his lump dick out of her pussy as he tried to get out from under her where he had been position. Now it was just Jenna and Mason.

"I'd like to get a taste of the sweet cunt," he said, pulling his dick from her ass.

They stood up and made their way to a chair in the corner. He saw Caleb pulling his cum dripping dick out of the girl's ass while Patrick was ramming inside her pussy.

"He must be about to cum," he thought to himself as he sat on the chair and stretched his arm out to Jenna. She hopped on top of his erect dick and began ride his dick. Her pussy was dripping wet with her cum and the load of cum Nathan had just released in her. Up and down she went on his dick, rocking back and forth occasionally. He flung his head back as if trying to take in all the ecstasy, licking his lips while giving her a hard smack on her ass. As he looked down at Jenna's beautiful melon-shaped breasts that seemed to be longing to be sucked, he gently brought his lips down to them and caressed the nipples with his tongue.

Jenna could hardly stop moaning, and the things she was saying when she was not moaning out were unbelievable. She kept begging him to fuck her dirty pussy and that she wanted that fucking dick inside her nasty little cunt. The more she spoke these strange yet erotic words, the more he could feel himself about to summit his climax. Finally, there was a loud groan, but it was not him, it was Patrick. As Mason turned his head to watch his friend, Jenna increased the motions that she was making with her pussy. Suddenly, he found Mason lost all control and with a few hard upwards thrust he too exploded inside her wicked pussy. He was not alone, the two other guys, Neil and Keith, had also come with loud groans inside the girl that they were fucking.

As the women searched the room for their clothing, the guys cleaned up and prepared to go downstairs to enjoy the rest of the party. It had definitely been an experience that Mason would not forget.

Saturday morning Mason woke up to the sound of his parents arguing. That had become the norm recently. His house seemed like a house of chaos where his parents acted like archenemies. As he laid in the bed, the argument continued, and when he could no longer stand to hear these two adults behave like teenagers, he got up, took his shower, and left. Over the last few months since he had joined the team, he had become incredibly close to Nathan, and as he drove around wondering what he should do, he decided to give Nathan a call.

"Yeah, man we can definitely hook up, I

was thinking we could go to strip club or something later." Nathan told him, in an effort to cheer him up and take his attention away from his arguing parents. He drove up to Nathan's home, and they spent the day, playing pool and drinking shots of vodka.

Later, as they made their way through the busy Saturday night traffic, Mason had two things on his mind, "titties and drinks." The bar was half-empty, and as they made their way to a front table, a petite blonde girl came to serve them, asking them what drinks they would like to order. They had more vodka as they looked on and enjoyed the show. Nathan's phone rang; it was Patrick on the other end, asking if he could join them. In less than ten minutes, Patrick showed up, and he had Caleb with him. The four friends sat at the table drinking and joking around. They joked about what had happened the previous night, and they all said that they would be delighted to have another wild night.

An idea popped in Nathan's mind. He shared his idea with the rest of the guys. Since they were in a strip bar, why not get one of the strippers to give them a private show?

"It's a slow night anyway, so she would be happy to get the extra cash," he added. The other guys agreed, and they tried to pick which stripper they would make their request to. Would it be the one dressed in the fire costume, or the night nurse, or even naughty professor? Finally, they decided to go with the naughty professor. They all agreed that this would be the best pick since they had all dreamed of fucking one of their professors.

Her stage name was Lilly, and she was a bit hesitant at first, but Nathan was an excellent negotiator and soon he was able to offer her a sweet deal.

"One would be surprised what a few hundred bucks can get you," he told the guys as he led them to a private room where the stripper was already waiting. She wore a blue dress and reading glasses, and her dark brown hair was pinned up in a ponytail. She almost looked she could have very well been a lecturer. As they sat down in the four chairs that had been placed in a semicircular position, she made her way to the door and ensured that it had been locked securely.

As Lilly strode across the room, the four guys looked on with curious eyes, not knowing what her next move would be. She made her way to the center of their semicircle and swayed her body from left to right to the rhythm of the music that was playing in the background. As she moved, she slowly began to undo the buttons of the dress that she wore, seductively slipping out of her only apparel. She had perfectly round breasts and a cute slender body. Mason was sure that both his hands could easily fit around her tiny waist. As she moved to the music, the guys found that they were moving to a different beat the throbbing of their now hardened dicks.

"Go ahead boys," she said, "You can all get some of this pussy for the right price," she continued as she parted her long legs and stroked the insides of her thighs.

They looked at each other, wondering if that

meant that they would get to fuck her. They all turned their attention to Nathan, the man with the money, who made things happen. A wicked little smile formed in the corner of his lips as he reached deep down into his pocket and pulled out a roll of hundreds. Mason almost screamed out with joy. It was definitely going down with the stripper. He braced himself for another wild erotic adventure with his teammates.

The horny guys looked on at the stripper as she caressed her breasts with her fingers; she began licking her lips and closing her eyes as she pleasured herself. Nathan was the first to whip out his dick and instruct her to suck it. She obliged to his request without asking any questions.

"Good girl," Nathan said as he gently patted her on the head, while she was down on her knees taking him in with her mouth. He stretched out his leg and tilted his head backward, a loud groan escaping his lips as she pleasured him with her tongue. Mason could see her head going up and down on his dick as she sucked his full length. The other guys were getting aroused from watching her give Nathan a blowjob, and soon, they all whipped out their dicks and began pleasuring themselves with long hard strokes on their hard dicks.

As Mason looked on, the desire to fuck Lilly increased, and soon, he was ready to get his share of the action.

"I want her on my dick," he said in a firm authoritative voice that had all the other guys shocked. Had it not been for the promise that he had made to him, Nathan would not have allowed the stripper to get off his dick. But he remembered that he had suggested going to the strip club to cheer Mason up, so Lilly made her way over to Mason, and with her back facing him, she glided her wet pussy down on his dick. He groaned at the feel of her wet flesh on his manhood. With her back against his chest, she ground her pussy on his dick; he could not resist the urge to fondle her breasts. The other guys watched as he took her nipples between two of his fingers and caressed them. Nathan got up out of his seat and had made his way in front of Mason.

Nathan stood there with his dick in his hand, waiting for Lilly to think of some innovative way to pleasure him. Finally, an idea crossed his mind; he held onto her head and brought it down to meet his erect dick. From where she was seated on Mason's dick, she could also suck his dick. He groaned at the pleasure that her tongue was bringing about on his cock, and he looked at the other guys with a look of arrogance on his face. Mason became turned on to a higher degree as he enjoyed the feelings from her riding his dick and view of her sucking Nathan's cock. She was amazing; he could sense that she was definitely more experienced than she looked.

The other two guys were using their hands to stroke their dicks, and their groaning seemed to cause Lilly to become aroused. She moved harder and faster against his dick, taking in Nathan with longer harder sucks. Her body was hot with passion, and Mason could feel her juices running down the full length of his dick. Fucking her was like plunging his dick into sweet ecstasy. As they fucked her, they noticed Nathan clenching his teeth and realized that he was now thrusting his dick inside Lilly's mouth.

With a loud groan, Nathan exploded his hot liquid inside her mouth. Before she had time to wipe his cum off her mouth, another dick was stuffed inside it. Patrick thrust his dick several times in her mouth, once even causing her to almost gag. He was the biggest of the four of them. Nonetheless, Lilly sucked his dick, using her tongue to caress every inch of it. Mason's attention was now captured by his own desire to pound her pussy even harder; he could feel his balls tightening and cum moving to the tip of his dick. With a loud moan, he gave her several hard upwards thrusts before ejaculating inside her pussy. He could feel tiny spasms running through her pussy, and the spasms, along with the loud moan that she gave, let him know that she too had reached her climax.

"C'mon man, I want to fuck her too, damn, get the fuck up," Caleb said with urgency in his voice. Just when Mason was about to get out of his seat, Patrick shot his load of cum in her mouth with a loud groan. Caleb rushed the other guys off to a corner and grabbed hold of Lilly by her ass. Bending her over him, he shoved his dick with full force inside her dripping wet pussy. It only took him a few good hard thrusts before he too exploded his juices inside her. Their bodies quivered, and he finally released her after a moment. The guys quickly got dressed as Nathan paid the stripper off, giving her a few extra hundreds for her great performance.

As they made their way to their cars, Mason received a call on his cell from Jenna. She and her friends were at a beach party, and they were wondering if he and his friends could join them.

"How many of your friends are there?" He asked curiously. She told him that it was her and three of her friends. Mason could not believe his luck; this weekend was turning out to be the best weekend of his life. They quickly made their way over to the beach where the girls were waiting. "Would it be another wild experience?" he wondered, as he made his way over to give Jenna a big hug.

"Glad to see you made it," she said to him. He smiled at her.

The pleasure will be all mine, I'm sure, he thought to himself, as he eyed his friends smiling at the other girls. Yep, they knew exactly what was about to go down.

7 SEDUCTIVELY DANGEROUS

Kenny had always had a crush on Mya but had always been too terrified of her boyfriend Salvatore to try for her. Salvatore was renowned for seriously injuring guys who tried to get with his girlfriend. Now that Salvatore, or Sal as he was called by many, had been locked up in prison, Kenny decided he would make his move on her. He had always had a good platonic relationship with her, and with Sal away, it was time to take their friendship to a new level. It was about seven in the evening when he called her.

Her voice on the phone sounded like she was lonely and desperately needing of love and affection. He had told her that he would come over to watch the movie she had picked out, but he had much more than that planned for tonight. Picking up a packet of three Trojan condoms and tucking them into his back pocket, he made his way over to her house.

She opened the door on the third or fourth knock. Kenny looked at her in astonishment, had she been on to him the entire time? She wore a sexy see-through white silk nightgown, which exposed almost all her cleavage. The gown stopped a few inches above her knees exposing her long slender legs, and her gorgeous figure was clearly visible through the thin fabric. As his gaze worked its way to the top of her beautiful body, he took in her attractive facial structure: her high cheeks bones and jawbone. Her hazel eyes seemed to pierce through his very soul as she looked at him, transferring a feeling a long and desire to him. She greeted him with a tight hug that allowed his body to feel her warmness and her soft breasts that lay bare under her gown. Kenny held on for a minute and he could feel an insanely powerful throbbing in his pants. He had gotten an erection at the very sight of her.

They went inside and she had a bottle of red wine on the coffee table along with a box of Dove chocolates. The coy little vixen, she had known all along that he wanted her, and although he had gone to her home to seduce her, it seemed like she would be the one doing the seducing. Kenny's eyes examined the inside of her small apartment, it was not much but everything was neatly placed, and it looked quite cozy. As he made his way to the couch, she took the remote and pointed it to her stereo. The sweet sound of soft music filled the air. The mood for the evening was definitely set and he was impressed with Mya, apparently, she had everything planned.

Mya popped open the bottle of red wine, holding up the two wine glasses in her hand as she poured both of them a full glass of red wine.

"Now that we have the red wine and the music going, we can watch this movie," she said as she handed him his wine.

He looked at her, and he could see a devious little smile form in the corner of her pink lips as she sipped on her drink. They chatted for a bit about the movie as it played, but before long they both were too wrapped in their feelings to continue dancing around their desires. Moving closer to him Mya locked her lips with his and their tongues lingered in a hot wet passionate kiss.

Kenny could not believe this was finally going to happen; they were going to make love. He used his hand to cup her face as he gave her several soft and gentle kisses each time tugging on her bottom lips, pulling it a little. Mya was definitely enjoying it because she did not resist him; instead, he felt her hands roaming wildly over his body.

"Oh God Mya, I wanted you so much, all this time, I've been waiting," he groaned as his feelings for her intensified with every kiss.

His hands made their way beneath her gown and it lifted to her chest area. Adjusting herself a little, she removed the gown and left her bare flesh exposed for him to pleasure. She was too tempting for him to resist; she was not even wearing any underwear. His eyes examined every inch of her completely naked body; he paid special attention to her clean-shaven pussy, giving her clitoris a few gentle strokes with his index finger. She moaned out in pleasure.

He moved his attention back to her upper body, taking in one of her perfectly round brown nipples in his mouth. His hot tongue caressed the nipple, sucking it gently and then licking it thoroughly. Again, she moaned out asking him to suck it harder. Upon hearing the urgency in her voice, Kenny increased the pressure of his tongue on her nipples, sucking longer and harder like she had requested. She closed her eyes and licked her lips while enjoying the feel of his tongue caressing her nipples. His dick throbbed and his erection increased; the blood was rushing down to his dick with massive force. He no longer wanted to fuck her, he needed to fuck her.

He felt her pulling against his touch so he stopped and she stood up, stretching her hands out to him before leading him into her bedroom. She invited him to lie down on the bed. As he lay down, she parted his long legs and positioned her head directly in contact with his erection. Kenny groaned as he felt her hot wet tongue licking his dick. She gently glided her tongue along the full length of his dick, taking in the entire thing in her mouth when she got to his head. Each stroke that she gave his dick sent shock waves through his body, and he found himself begging her for more.

"Yeah girl, don't stop, just like that, don't stop," he said as he closed his eyes and enjoyed the moment.

Taking hold of the head of his dick in her mouth, she flicked her tongue back and forth and then used her tongue to create small circular motions along the edge of the head.

The more she sucked, the closer he came exploding his load of cum in her mouth. He tried hard to control himself, and finally in an effort to try to hold back, he pulled her head away from his dick, took a deep breath, and then instructed her to lie down in the same position he had been laying in. He wanted to give her a taste of her own medicine. He decided that he would suck her pussy and drive her wild the same way she had used her tongue on his dick. As she positioned herself on the bed, he spread her legs far apart and placed a pillow under her ass to prop up her pussy. Now that he had her exactly how he wanted, he used his fingers and stroked her pussy while staring directly into her beautiful brown eyes. He could see the desire building up, and it excited him much more than she could have imagined.

Kenny leaned in and used his tongue to stroke her pussy. Her flesh was hot and wet; although it was chocolate brown on the outside, it was pretty pink on the inside. He indulged in eating her pussy out, his face buried deep as he licked and sucked her raw flesh. She moaned and her body tensed up as he pleasured her thoroughly with his tongue. Her hands ran through his hair as she whispered profanities to him. He stroked her pussy gently with his tongue while using his finger to penetrate her insides. His tongue found its way to her clitoris, and he gave it several long hard sucks, causing her to dig her fingers into the sheets as her legs shook uncontrollably.

Yes, he was definitely pleasuring her exactly how she had pleasured him.

After a while, he could no longer suppress the desire to stick his dick deep down in her sweet, wet pussy. He stroked his huge member a few times before thrusting it inside her. A loud shriek escaped her lips; she had been so consumed with the sweet stroking of his tongue that she had forgotten about his huge cock. He penetrated her flesh, over and over, giving her slow strokes at first but then increasing his momentum with shorter, quicker, and harder thrusts. Her tiny bed rocked violently as he thrust his dick with full force inside her pussy. She wrapped her legs his around his waist while she moaned in pleasure, enjoying every inch of his dick.

"Don't stop, baby, please," she moaned as she licked her lips and closed her eyes.

He fucked her over and over and her pussy seemed to beg for more of his hard thrusts. Kenny lost himself inside her warm cunt and exploded inside her, with a loud groan. He looked down at her and saw the look of satisfaction on her face. She had also climaxed and her body shook as she tried to calm down. He could feel both their juices running out of her pussy and onto his dick.

Fucking her had been everything he had hoped it would have been, and much more. She had a tight little pussy that he enjoyed pounding. As he had fucked her, he could feel tiny spasms running through her pussy that caused what felt like contractions on his dick. He gave her a few more slow strokes with his dick to ensure that he had released all his semen in her; then the two of them lay in each other's arms where they finally dozed off into deep sleep.

As they lay in bed the following morning, there was a loud banging on her door. They immediately woke up and looked at each other with curiosity-filled eyes. Was it the cops?

They did not know. They had both fallen asleep naked; Mya got up and looked around her room for something to slip into before going to the door. She found a pink bathrobe and quickly put it on before going over to open the front door. Kenny got out of the bed and walked towards the bedroom to hear who was at the door.

"What are you doing here?" he heard Mya say. "How'd you get out?" she asked again. Although he could not quite make out the entire conversation, he heard when Mya almost shouted that she was just taking a shower and he heard the voices drawing closer to the bedroom. He quickly made his way to the back of her closet and shut the door quietly as he peeped through the small cracks in the closet door.

Kenny's heart almost skipped a beat when he saw the all too familiar face that had entered the bedroom with her. It was Salvatore. Kenny was puzzled because the last thing he had heard was that he had been picked up by the police and sent to prison for numerous charges ranging from trafficking and distributing drugs to assault with deadly weapon.

Sal was a tough, rugged looking man, probably in his late thirties, much older than Mya and even older than Kenny himself. He had dark grey eyes and a scar on the right side of his face. Kenny knew that this man was dangerous, and if he were to be caught by Sal, he would be good as dead. He looked once more and saw Mya's face and he wondered why she wasn't scared; she simply stood there, with an expressionless look on her face.

Again, he heard her questioning Sal about how he had gotten out of jail.

"Why you asking all these questions? I'm out ain't I? I didn't break out but am here and I paid for this apartment, so stop with all the fucking questions already," Sal said.

Clearly he was getting irritated by Mya's constant questions. Upon hearing his answer, Mya did not ask any more questions.

"Well I am just about to go take my shower to get ready for work," she said walking away from him towards the bathroom.

Kenny watched her as she entered the bathroom, and he found himself praying harder than he had ever prayed before, begging God to get him out of the mess he was in. He even promised to stay away from Mya if he were able to escape out of his hiding spot without being seen.

Kenny looked on and when Mya got out of the bathroom, he experienced the most uncomfortable situation he had ever been in. Sal had pulled off her bathrobe and had begun kissing and caressing her neck. How could she allow him to do that after they had just spent a night of passion together? Sal was undressing himself as he kissed her; the entire time, Mya did not show any resistance. She was moaning and closing her eyes enjoying his touches.

Soon they were both naked lying on the bed in missionary position. He could see Mya's tiny body under Sal's heavy masculine body as he penetrated the insides of her flesh. He was groaning and saying profanities to her as he fucked her hard. The squeaking that the spring in the bed made got louder and louder as Sal's thrusts got harder and harder. One time Kenny almost leaped out of the closet to help Mya, fearing that she was seriously in terrible pain. Her cries sounded like she was in pure hell. Then all of a sudden, Sal's thrusts became slower and gentler, and Kenny saw Mya's hand grip hard against Sal's ass as she begged him to fuck her harder. The little devil. She had been enjoying the rough sex all along. The more Kenny looked on, the more he could feel his own dick becoming harder and harder. At first, he thought the entire thing was disgusting but it was actually very pleasurable; it was like watching porn. In fact, it was better; it was live action, a few inches away from him. He quietly whipped out his erect dick and began stroking it gently.

Sal rolled over while Mya mounted. She looked gorgeous; her skin looked hot and sweaty. And as she got on top of his dick, he groaned out with pleasure. Up and down she bounced on his dick and rocked her body back and forth occasionally. She was riding his dick with so much vigor and energy Kenny almost forgot that Sal was in the room; he too wanted his share of her pussy. He realized that she was saying stuff to Sal. Leaning in closer the door where Kenny listened attentively, trying to make out what she was saying.

"OH, motherfucker, yeah, shit, fuck that little pussy. You missed it didn't you?" Mya said as she rode Sal's dick hard, banging her pussy against the full length of his dick.

Kenny could not believe his ears; she was just as dirty with her words as he was. Sweat slowly trickled down the sides of his face as he desperately longed to get release. However, he knew that it would be impossible to ejaculate in the closet without any one hearing him, so he tried his best to suppress his impending climax.

Sal gave her several hard smacks on her ass, causing her to moan out loud. As he smacked her, he was thrusting upwards inside her pussy, harder than before. She continued riding his dick and finally with a loud moan she released. Her climax was soon followed by Sal's loud groans as he released his come inside her pussy. Kenny clenched his teeth, trying to prevent his own climax.

After a few minutes of cuddling, Sal got up put his clothes on and told her he would be back in a few hours.

As soon as he heard the door close, Kenny burst the doors of the closet opening, launching across the living room to where Mya was locking up to the front door. He had his throbbing dick in his hand and he felt like he would explode if he did not get to cum. In a swift move, he quickly bent Mya over with her hand stretched as she braced against the door for support. He gave a hard powerful thrust in her already wet pussy. At that moment he did not care that it was already filled up with Sal's cum; he just wanted to release his inside her.

Kenny thrust his dick inside her again, this time harder and faster than he had done before. Her ass bounced back against his groin area and he closed his eyes and gave her several hard thrusts. She moaned out, begged him to stop. Her pussy was swollen from the dick she had been getting between last night and this morning. However, her pleas fell on deaf ears as he thrust himself in her with all his might. Soon, what had been pleas of resistance turned into moans of pleasure, and she began begging him to fuck her harder. In and out he slammed his huge dick. Her body jerked forward every time as tiny ripples ran through her ass cheeks. He could not resist the urge to smack her. As he fucked her with his dick, his palm came crashing down her bare flesh giving her several loud smacks.

"Yeah, fuck my wet pussy, smack that ass, baby," she moaned as she rocked her booty to the rhythm of his thrusts.

She was turning him on even more with her dirty talk. His thrust became harder and harder, and he found himself now saying profanities to her. "You want that cock, bounce that ass against it, yeah, bounce it baby." He gave her thrust after thrust and she moaned for more. Finally, when he could not hold back any more, he released all of himself. His hot liquid pulsed inside of her pussy, and she moaned out asking him to leave his dick in her as she proceeded to use her fingers to rub against her clitoris. Within a matter of seconds, she reached her climax and gave a loud moan as she released her juices unto his dick.

Now both of them had released and her case, she had gotten to cum two times in one morning, with two different men. They sat on the couch exhausted and dripping wet with sweat and cum. As they sat there, Kenny used that quiet time to find out exactly what her intensions were, what this would mean for their friendship. And of course with Sal back at home, did that mean that they were going to get back together. All his questions seem to overwhelm her, and she took a deep breath before answering. She explained that Sal was very dangerous and not the type of man he wanted to make mad. The look in her eyes told him that she was not in love with Sal, what she felt was pure fear. She was terrified of this man and what he could do to her.

The car she drove, the apartment she lived in, and even the clothes that she wore were all paid for with his money. He practically owned her, and as much as she would have loved to just break up with him and start a new life with Kenny, she knew he would never allow it. Sal was a very dangerous man and the mere fact that he felt like he owned her made her equally dangerous because any man who tried to get with her would have to go through Sal first.

"Well I don't care about Sal," Kenny said with a sound of foolish bravery in his voice. "Whatever he can dish out I can handle," he continued as he planted a soft kiss on her forehead. He used the back of his hand to wipe away the thin line of tears that were now making their way down the side of her face.

She sniffed a little and smiled, "Really?" she said holding his hand and bringing it to her mouth for a gently kiss. "Well we need to find a way to get rid of Sal for good," she said. The look of sadness that she had on her face now changed as a wicked little smile formed in the cresses of her pink lips.

Kenny leaned back in his seat and closed his eyes thinking to himself. What did she mean by get rid of? Could she be just as dangerous as Sal?

No, she was worse; she was seductively dangerous. Kenny knew that he would do anything for her; all she had to do was ask him.

8 MOON, STARS AND HIS BIG BLACK STICK

Patty rolled over in their huge bed and looked across to her husband's side of the bed. Leo looked so peaceful as he slept she almost felt guilty leaving the house in the middle of the night. As she looked over to the nightstand, she could see his cell phone blinking and she knew that it must have been one of his mistresses, texting or calling him. Their marriage had almost reached its breaking point because of Leo's lust for other women. At night they slept in the same bed but they hardly ever touched each other. During the day, their home was chaotic with constant loud arguments. She had endured years of what seemed like torture in an unhappy marriage.

But now things had begun to look brighter for her. She had a hot, young lover that she was about to sneak out of the house to go meet. Her husband had done the same for years with tons of younger women. Now it was payback time. She was doing the exact same thing he did to her.

Patty quietly slipped out of the bed, being sure not to make any sudden movements, and walked over to their bathroom. She applied a light shade of red lipstick and changed into the sexy red lace lingerie she had bought especially for Jason, her twenty-two year old lover. Both Patty and her husband were in their late thirties; at first, it had felt a little weird for her to be dating a man who was so much younger than herself. As she prepared herself for tonight, she soon forgot everything about their age and swiftly made her way to the front door. Making sure that no one was watching, Patty quickly made her way down the block to where Jason had been waiting in his black mustang convertible. He had the top dropped down, and as they drove, her beautiful blonde hair sailed with the wind.

Jason looked strikingly handsome; he was a well-built young man. His dark chocolate complexion was the total opposite of her creamy pale complexion, and their differences made her all the more attracted to him. Tonight they had planned a midnight picnic in the backyard of his one bedroom mobile home. He drove off the main road onto a small private road. Along the way she could see a few other mobile homes, but they were all a good distance away from each other. Finally, they got to his home. He parked his car on the side of the house and rushed out to open her door. He held her hand as he led her to the front door. "Welcome to my humble abode," he said as he stepped inside and invited her to follow him.

She was somewhat impressed; she had never been inside a mobile home. In fact, she always looked down at mobile homes, thinking that they were cramped little boxes that weren't actually comfortable enough to be a suitable home for anyone. It was actually very spacious inside. He had very little furniture; a computer desk and chair were the only furniture she saw in his living room area. Her eyes caught sight of a beautiful fruit basket on the kitchen counter. He must have prepared it for tonight, she thought as she walked over to where it was.

Jason crept up from behind, surprising her with a warm embrace while gently rocking her from side to side, as he playfully planted tiny kisses on the sides of her cheeks. She blushed. She felt like a teenager all over again.

Taking hold of the basket, he led her to his beautiful backyard. They sat on the soft green grass and engaged in lively conversation. The talked about everything – their childhood, their cars, and school. Soon they were exhausted from talking, and Patty lay back facing the beautiful sky, staring up at the stars and the full moon. It was such a romantic night. Soon the beautiful view that she had been enjoying was disrupted as Jason's lip came crashing down on hers, in a hot, wet, passionate kiss. Patty did not resist him. Their tongues danced together in the sweet ecstasy of the moment.

His mouth left hers and made its way down

her body, caressing the nape of her neck. Slowly he began undressing her, rolling down the red tube dress she wore. Her breasts were bare; she had not worn a bra. He carefully sucked on her right nipple while his finger flicked the left one. She moaned. The pleasure she was feeling was intense and the fact that she could see the beautiful sky as she looked up made it seem magical. Over and over his tongue lavished her nipples, giving them soft gentle strokes and then sucking on them hard. Patty could feel her pink lace thong becoming saturated from her arousal. Although he was young, the way he caressed her body left her thinking he was an experienced lover.

His mouth moved away from her nipples and trailed along her body, finally stopping at its destination, her pussy. She gasped when she felt his hot tongue sweep through her pussy in a single lingering stroke. He was licking the insides of her pink flesh and sending shivers through her body. It had been a while since anyone had pleasured her down there, and Patty found it hard to control her emotions. She found her eyes tearing up as she moaned out to him, begging him to stick his tongue inside her whole. Her pleas fell on deaf ears; Jason was his own man, not willing to be controlled by any woman. He pleasured her the way he wanted, in long slow strokes. His tongue then moved upward to her clit. Gently he gripped it with his mouth, giving it several hard sucks. Occasionally, he flicked his tongue on the tip of her clit; Patty really enjoyed when he would do that.

As he sucked her pussy, his hands followed the direction his tongue had taken. Slipping in one finger at a time, he began to penetrate her insides with rapid thrusts. Patty closed her eyes as she enjoyed the most intense feeling she had ever experienced. Her heart thudded as tiny spasms made their way to her pussy and her juices flowed like a fountain. He licked, sucked, and finger fucked her pussy and seemed to enjoy doing it. Her body cringed and her fingers dug into the green grass, capturing a handful of grass when he suddenly plunged his tongue inside her moist center. "Oh, Jason," she moaned as she tore out handfuls of grass.

Patty could feel her impending climax as Jason continued to thrust his tongue inside her pussy and licked her juices every time he pulled his tongue out. She gave a long, loud moan as tremors ran through her body, twisting and turning her legs. She finally released and exploded on his tongue. He was more than thrilled to see her cum; he licked her juices to the very last drop, making pleasurable sounds as he went along.

Now that she had been satisfied, she wanted to take him in and pleasure him with her tongue the way he had pleasured her. He did not resist. He positioned himself, lying down on the grass, as she parted his legs and captured his erect dick with her mouth. His dick had a beautiful dark chocolate tone, and it was definitely bigger than her husband's. Huge bulging veins ran across it and it had a big, round purple head at the top. As her lips went down around him, he groaned out loud;

it was like she found encouragement in his moans because she increased the momentum of her sucks. Her tongue lavished across his dick, and he used his hand to grasp the back of her head controlling her movements.

The more she sucked his dick, the harder it became and after a while, it had almost doubled in size. Her sucks were hard and long at first but then changed to shorter, quicker sucks. She flicked her tongue over the top of his head and then traced it the edge of the head of his massive cock. Jason groaned as she pleasured him, her tongue running wildly over his entire dick. She could have done this until he ejaculated, but she wanted to feel his dick inside her wet pussy. With one long hard suck, she pulled her mouth away from his raw meat. He looked like he almost had a heart attack when she stopped; the look of longing in his eyes was undeniable.

Patty rolled over to his side and parted her legs, motioning him to come stick his dick inside her waiting cunt. He did not hesitate. A loud shriek escaped her lips as she felt the full force of his dick as he penetrated her insides. His eyes lit up as he felt her tightness on his flesh. "Wow, you're real tight!" he said, as he continued to thrust deeper and deeper inside her. Patty now found herself wishing that she had continued sucking his dick, this pressure that she felt was too intense. In fact, she felt like her pussy was being ripped apart. His thrusts had increased to hard banging. Over and over, he plunged his dick viciously inside her pussy without stopping. She was begging him to go slower, not so hard and fast. Her attention was soon captured by the view of the stars and the moon that she had as she laid there on her back being fucked. Somehow, the serenity of the sky brought about a more pleasurable feeling, and she was now begging him for more. It was not bad at all. It was amazing. He had a huge, sweet, long dick that pleasured her the way no man had pleasured her before.

As they continued fucking, Patty's entire demeanor changed and she now found herself whispering obscenities in his ears, gripping his body and enjoying the ride. His thrusts sent shockwaves through her, and she was now wet all over again. His dick seemed to be going deep down inside her, so deep that it was banging against her pussy walls. "O yeah, fuck, yeah, fuck me!" she moaned as he closed his eyes and fucked her harder. They were hot and sweaty, and the ecstasy that they felt was amazing. Each thrust caused her to moan out loud. Occasionally, he would slow down a little and give her some slow long strokes, but after a few seconds, he would pick up the pace again and give her several hard thrusts.

Patty felt her pussy contracting violently, and she had to take deep breaths to calm herself. The view in the sky was so pleasant and it felt so right, yet here they were in the backyard, doing something so wrong. As his momentum increased once more, she gripped his shoulders hard, and with a loud moan, she had another great orgasm. His eyes locked gazes with hers, and it was like she transferred everything she had been feeling onto him. He gave her several long hard thrust and finally gave a loud groan. "Oh shit! I'm gonna cummm," he groaned as his hot liquid exploded inside of her pussy. His shook violently as he tried to control his breathing and calm down.

After a while, he rolled over to her side, and they both lay outside in the aftermath of their ecstasy, enjoying the view of the sky.

Eventually, Patty sat up and asked Jason to drop her off back at her house. Although she did not really care about her husband, she did not want him waking up to an empty bed. The drive back to the house was one of few words but lots of emotions and feelings. She was beginning to deeply care for this young man. She could tell from the way he looked at her and spoke to her that he felt the same way about her. When she got back to the house, she silently crept back into bed while her unsuspecting husband was still asleep.

Today was her birthday and Patty had plans for tonight with a special man. That man was not her husband; it was Jason. She had booked a suite at a hotel, and she had told Leo that she would be going out with some girlfriends in the evening. As she sat in her car, stuck in the afternoon traffic, images of the night she had spent with Jason continued to play over and over in her mind. Yes, she was definitely looking forward to tonight. Her phone rang and it was Jason –

this was about the fourth time he had called for the day. This time he was just confirming the date. He was such a nice guy; never in her wildest dreams did she ever think that he would be so mature for his age.

As she opened the door, her eyes nearly popped out of the sockets in disbelief. Her house was adorned with red roses and candles everywhere. What was going on? Was Leo planning on having one of his mistresses over? She wandered through the house from room to room trying to find him. Finally, she found him upstairs in their bathroom filling up the Jacuzzi.

"What's going on Leo? Why you preparing shit for your women in my home?" she shot out angrily.

He looked tentatively at her before replying that he had done all these things for her. He knew that they weren't really getting along, but it was her birthday and he still cared about her. Patty could feel her knees getting week as she remembered that in the past they had always spent their birthdays together. Now that she had a new man in her life, this tradition had completely slipped her mind.

"Well, I don't know what to say," she said as she remembered that Jason was probably on his way to the hotel already. What a mess she had gotten herself into.

Seeing that he had probably gone through a lot of trouble to prepare for tonight, she decided that she would stay a few minutes, have a few bites to eat, and drink a little wine with her husband. She went upstairs to take her shower, and she came back downstairs dressed in the outfit she had planned to go out in. She saw a look in his eyes that she had not seen in a while; it was the look of desire. He wanted her; she could feel it, hear it in his tone of voice, and see it in his stares. Even looking down at the crotch of his pants, she could see the bulge from his erect penis.

She sat down and enjoyed the beautiful dinner he had prepared. The entire time her phone kept vibrating, and she knew it was Jason on the phone. Finally, she excused herself and went to the bathroom. She called Jason and lied through her teeth, telling him that her mom and some of her friends had planned a surprise party for her and that she could not leave just yet. She promised that she would be there with him tonight but it might just be later than they had planned. "Order room service and watch some TV, I'll be over as soon as I can," she said as they ended their conversation.

She went back to the dining room where Leo was waiting. They had a few more drinks and soon she found herself on the table with Leo's mouth devouring hers. They were hot for each other and could not control themselves. They were ripping each other's clothes away as their lips locked in a deep passionate kiss. She wanted to resist him, but her body could not. The pleasure that she felt was so intense that she soon found her hand roaming over his body in search of his erection. When she found it, she gently stroked it, while he took hold of her breasts with his mouth, sucking each nipple slowly.

The more he sucked her nipples, the more

she wanted to feel his cock inside her hot wet pussy. Soon she guided it the point of penetration. He welcomed her gesture, and without thinking twice, he penetrated her pussy with his long dick. She tensed up a little as his dick made its way deeper and deeper inside her sweet pussy. A soft moan escaped her tender lips, and he covered it with his hot, desire-filled lips.

He gave her a combination of strong, long thrusts and shorter, harder thrusts. The plates on the table rattled and fell to the floor as they used the table as if it were a bed. He grabbed hold of her breasts with his lips once again, and as he fucked her, his tongue licked and sucked her nipples, pleasuring her even further. She thought she would lose her mind. This was the man that she had not been getting along with for the past couple of months; now it had seemed like they had been perfect lovers. Over and over, his dick penetrated her moist heat, and soon she found herself at the brink of her climax. Gripping hard onto the edge of the table, she closed her eyes and lost herself in the ecstasy of the moment. Her climax was immense and her juices flowed like it was an everlasting stream. Upon seeing her release and feeling her wetness on his cock, Leo too gave a few hard thrusts and let out a loud groan, exploding a sea of his hot cum inside her. They both had reached an incredible climax. They lay on the table for a while trying to figure out what had just happened between them.

As Patty got off the table, she remembered

that Jason was already at the suite waiting for her. She quickly made up another lie, this time to tell her husband. She took a quick shower before leaving for the hotel.

Thankfully, the highway was not very busy, and she reached her destination in less than twenty minutes. She swiftly made her way to the elevator and made her way to the fifth floor where she had booked Suite No. 122.

After the third knock, Jason came to the door wearing nothing but his red boxer shorts. She walked in past him and she was amazed to see that there was table adorned with red roses and a bottle of red wine on the patio outside. They made their way to the patio and had some lively conversation while sipping the wine. As they stood there watching the view from the patio, Patty could feel the space between them getting smaller. Jason was now standing behind her cuddling her in his strong arms. She moaned when she felt his hot tongue suddenly make contact with the nape of her neck. She turned around and their lips meet in a hot, passionate kiss. He was groaning and she could tell that he was horny by the way he was running his hands wildly all over her body.

He braced her up against the patio wall and was kissing her while his hand slowly undressed her. She, too, found herself undressing him. Soon her hands roamed to his groin area; she cupped his dick with her hands. Slowly she dropped down to her knees and took him into her mouth. She used her tongue to pleasure every inch of his long dick. His hands were stroking the back of her hair as her tongue moved all over his cock. When she got to the head, she took a few minutes to caress it, flicking her tongue all over it and sucking hard on it. His head fell backward as a loud groan escaped his lips.

When he could no longer handle the intensity of her hot tongue on his dick, he pulled her upward and captured her lips with a soft, long kiss. She moaned and before she could open her eyes, he had turned her around. He quickly bent her over the railings, parted her ass cheeks, and proceeded to penetrate her pussy from the back. She moaned as his dick made its way into her swollen pussy. The fact that she had just had sex less than two hours ago made her feel a little guilty at first. Would he be able to tell she thought to herself, as he gave her several slow, long thrusts? As she was being fucked, she realized that she could see the moon and stars. Every stroke reminded her of the night when they had made love on the grass in his backyard.

It had been a beautiful night and here she was culminating it all by taking in his huge cock as she enjoyed the amazing view. Over and over he pounded her pussy, each thrust harder than the last. Soon enough he gave a loud groan and exploded inside her pussy. She also reached her climax. He remained inside her for a while as they both admired the moon and the stars that lit up the sky.

9 MAESTRO UNLEASHED

"I'm Señor Raul, el maestro. Which translates to I'm your professor," Raul said to his class of about thirty senior college students.

It was his first day of teaching and he had been very nervous about their reception towards him. He feared that they would not respect him since he was a twenty-six-year-old teaching a group of students in their early twenties. As he looked around the class, he saw that majority of his students were attractive young women. He felt like a hungry lion at a zoo, seeing possible prey but unable to chase it down and eat it.

After a few minutes into his class, the door flew open and the most attractive woman he had ever seen walked in. She had a beautiful chocolate brown complexion that was the exact opposite of his creamy pale complexion, and he liked it. She made her way to the front of the class and asked to talk to him privately for a moment. He took her aside and she handed him a formal letter and explained that she was a transfer student from Jamaica. She had a strong native accent, and he found himself leaning in closer to her to try to make out exactly what she was saying. As he leaned in, the sweet fragrance of her perfume drifted to his nose. She smelled like sweet lilies with a hint of island breeze. Maybe it was all in his head, but there was something about her that had him enthralled. He longed to be with her in every possible way.

That evening, when he went home to his lonely house, the thought of her consumed him. He had gotten aroused by just thinking about her, and it was not just her good looks—he loved her exotic Jamaican accent. He didn't understand why he was feeling like that. He thought long and hard, trying to find a plausible reason for his fascination of her. His dick throbbed, and he needed a release. He wondered if he should call his ex-girlfriend but decided not to, as it would just start up some unnecessary drama. Desperate, he made his way over to his computer. He browsed through the porn website, trying to search a video with a girl that looked similar to his new crush.

A caption caught his attention: "island babe with dick in ass." Raul quickly clicked on the link to the video and unzipped the crotch of his pants. He got comfortable in his chair and hit the play button at the bottom of the screen. He whipped out his dick and gave it some long hard strokes as he looked on with gluttonous eyes.

The girl in the video had the same chocolate brown complexion as his student. He watched the video girl walking along the pristine beach, and he was actually startled when the huge dark-haired man came up from behind her. He grabbed her by waist and pulled her against his lean muscular body.

A little dirty talk passed between the two; the words actually turned Raul on as did the moment when their lips made contact and they began passionately kissing each other.

Little by little, they began slipping off each other's clothes. Raul adjusted himself in the chair he was seated in, parting his legs further and gaining better access to his erect dick. He used circular motions on his dick as he worked his way from the base of his penis all the way up to the head. He groaned out loud, as he imagined that it was him in the video with the sexy vixen. His gaze intensified as he pleasured himself.

The woman in the video bent over with her hands and knees in the sand, while the man stroked his dick in preparation; then, he penetrated her from the back. As his dick made its way inside her pussy, the camera focused on the point of entry. Raul could clearly see her tiny little hole expanding to accommodate the guy's huge cock. When the dick was fully inside her, he pulled it out again and gave her a quicker thrust. She moaned out loud and at the same time Raul groaned as he increased the momentum with which he was stroking his dick. Again, the camera focused on the penetration point and showed the hardened dick moving in and out of her pussy. Raul was enjoying the show, so he put it on slow motion as he continued his hand job.

Onscreen the girl moaned and begged the guy to fuck her harder. Finally, he pulled out and used his hard dick to give her a few smacks across her firm, round ass. Looking back at the top of the video where the name was, Raul realized that the guy was about to fuck her in the ass, just like the name had suggested. The man used his saliva to lubricate his dick and her asshole before penetrating her from the back. She gave a loud shriek as her body jerked forward at the impact of his first thrust. Somehow, the camera had been positioned between the man's legs, and her anus was in clear view, allowing Raul to watch as the dick forced its way through her tiny hole. The camera changed its focus and captured the expression on the woman's face. She had her eyes closed tight and she clenched her teeth; her fingers dug into the sand as he gave her several hard thrusts. With each mighty thrust, her body moved forward a little and she closed her eyes even tighter, opening them occasionally while she took deep breaths. The camera soon focused on the man's face, and Raul could see his desire-filled eyes light up every time she moaned out. Before long, the camera was back shooting from the point of entry angle, showing every thrust that he made. He had increased his thrusts and was literally pounding her anus with his long dick.

She moaned uncontrollably and Raul felt

his blood boil as the throbbing in his dick increased. As her body twisted and turned and her moans grew louder, the intensity of Raul's pleasure increased. He gripped his dick tightly and stroked his full length viciously with the palm of his hand. For a moment, he lost himself in his desires and his hot liquid shot out of his dick, splattering all over his computer desk and keyboard. As he calmed himself down and took some deep breaths, he noticed the man in the video had also increased the momentum of his thrusts. Soon the man gave a loud groan accompanied by a mighty thrust and exploded inside the woman's anus.

Taking a long deep breath, Raul hit the stop button at the bottom of the screen. The video still had about twenty minutes more.

"My God, what else would these people do? The guy had already ejaculated," he thought to himself as he made his way over to the bathroom to wipe his wet dick.

As the weeks went by, Raul's attraction for his student only became stronger. Initially he had thought he would be able to control himself, but this had proved to be a difficult challenge as she had been wearing some really provocative clothes to class. Each day he would wait till all the students had left the class before standing up from behind his desk. He was sure that they would notice his erect dick piercing through his pants if he were to stand in front of them.

When he got home, it was even worse; he found himself masturbating upon the thought of fucking that girl every single day. Sometimes he even masturbated twice—once when he got home and when he was in bed just before falling asleep. It was almost like she had put a spell on him and he just could not get her out of his mind.

That day she had worn black leggings that hugged perfectly her body, showing her voluptuous figure. The top part of her outfit was a tight tank top with a deep "V" cut, exposing her tempting cleavage. She sat in the front row, and he could not keep his eyes off her; in fact, he caught her giving him little seductive stares every time their eyes met. She must have known what she was doing to him. His dick had begun throbbing, and he honestly had thought that he could have ejaculated by just staring at her cleavage long enough.

As he made his way inside his house after what seemed like the longest day of his life, he rushed over to his computer. He was going to indulge in some hardcore porn that evening. However, to his surprise, the porn was just not cutting it tonight. He needed pussy, real pussy, and he needed it immediately. Picking up his phone hesitantly, he called the only person he knew that he could probably get pussy from on such a short notice.

His ex-girlfriend, Amanda, was thrilled to hear his voice, and it took her less than twenty minutes to arrive at his house. As he opened the door to let her in, he had one thing on his mind—sex.

"I knew you'd want me back," she said with an arrogant look on her face. She was sure she knew him well. Unbeknownst to her, he just wanted a quick release and had no intentions of getting back with her.

He did not even make any comments on her remark. In a swift movement, he had her back planted against the wall as his tongue devoured hers in a hot wet kiss. She moaned out and he planted a series of kisses all over her neck. His hand made its way under her blouse. She was not wearing any bra, and he took that as an invitation to suck her nipples. His tongue went wild, sucking and licking each nipple, one at a time. As he sucked her nipples, his hand stroked her long legs and soon made its way up her thighs, ripping her thin thong away from her flesh. She moaned again, that time with more vigor as he stroked the insides of her pussy with his fingers.

"You're so wet," he moaned as he continued to pleasure her with his tongue. She swallowed hard, unable to comment. The intensity of his strokes caused her body to quiver as tiny spasms rushed through her body.

Suddenly he felt her soft palm cupping his hard dick. He had been so engrossed in sucking her nipples and finger fucking her that he hadn't noticed when she had unzipped his pants. Her warm feminine caress caused him to part his lips from her as a loud groan escaped his lips. Her strokes were different from his: they were tender and delicate, but still had the same intense effect. His dick throbbed; he now wanted to penetrate her more than anything else at that moment.

When he could no longer control himself, he pulled her hand away from his cock and released her nipples. He turned her around so that she was now facing the wall. Taking both her hands in his, he placed them on the wall as he encouraged her to brace against the wall for support. He entered her from behind just like how the guy in the porn video did. She shrieked out in pain as he penetrated her wet pussy.

"Oh God, yeah, baby," she moaned as he continued his upward thrust inside her pussy.

Once his full length was inside her, he began steadily thrusting in and out of her hot core. Her ass was like a soft cushion, and as he fucked her, visions of what he had seen in the video kept playing in his mind. He was going wild and his thrusts increased from slow, steady thrust to hard, rough penetrations. She moaned and moaned while he fucked her. He felt like he would explode anytime; her pussy was just as sweet as he remembered. Finally, with a long hard thrust, they both climaxed and released their juices.

"Wow, that was amazing," she said, looking at him, waiting for a positive response.

"Yeah, it was," he replied.

Reality was hitting him; he had just opened up a can of worms by fucking her. He made up some excuse about having to go pick up his mom from work because her car was down just to get her out of his house. He did not mean to be mean, but he also did not want to start anything with her again. He had a feeling he would be hearing from her again pretty soon. She was not the "hit it and quit it" type of girl.

A few weeks had gone by and surprisingly he had not heard from his ex-girlfriend, Amanda. He now found himself wondering about her and why she hadn't tried to call or see him yet. Finally, after much hesitation, he picked up his cell phone and dialed her number.

"Hello, hello!" she said in a panting voice. "What? I can't hear you," she continued.

It sounded like she was having sex and now pretending that she could not hear. His suspicion was confirmed when he heard a male voice in the background groaning and then the bed squeaking. "I can't hear anything," she said as she abruptly ended the call. He tried calling her back, but calls went straight to her voicemail. She had switched off her phone.

This was unbelievable—the one person he thought would be available anytime for some hot sex was now actually having some hot sex without him. Angry for no reason, Raul proceeded to masturbate before bed, but for some reason, he just could not get the right movie, nor could he get the right touch. Overall, he was just unable to satisfy himself tonight. He went to bed sad, lonely, and horny.

It was the day of final exams, and as Raul walked around the class monitoring the students to ensure that there was no cheating or copying, his eyes locked gazes with a guilty student. It was the Jamaican girl, Kathy. He pulled her off to the side of the class, and as he spoke to her, his eyes fell on the writing in the palm of her hand. She had several Spanish words and their English translations scribbled on her hand. He could not believe this; he had never caught anybody cheating before. He did not want to fail her automatically because of her cheating, and so he sent her off to the washroom to clean her hands. When she returned, he carefully examined her palms before allowing her to continue. He told her that she would need to come to his office after the exam, as she had just committed a serious offense that could possibly lead to suspension from school.

After the exam, she came to his office just like he had instructed her. She hung her head down in shame. As he sat in his chair, his eyes carefully examined every inch of her body. She had a casual black dress on, but it was super short. He wanted to just bend her over and fuck her right there on his desk. However, he tried to remove the thoughts out of his mind. He tried to find out why she did what she just did. Then, he told her about the penalties that she could face.

Before he could even continue, she burst

into tears. She cried bitterly as she begged him to forgive her and overlook her mistake in judgment. She told him that she was there on a scholarship and her mom had worked two jobs just to send her and the rest of her siblings to school.

"Them gone take away me scholarship," she said in her Jamaican accent. The more she pleaded with him, the hornier he found himself becoming; he now had a full-blown arousal. "Me gone do anything Sir, anything, jus doe tell them noting pun de test."

Suddenly he realized what was going on— she was trying to seduce him. Her begging was done in a very sly and manipulative type of way. She was now a few inches away from him, and as he looked into her eyes, he saw a little devious look. She was up to mischief and he was weirdly turned on by her attitude.

"You will do anything I say, right?" he asked as he moved closer to her; now they could feel each other's breath on their skin.

Her lips came crashing on his as she engaged him in a deep passionate kiss. He pulled away and then he walked over to lock the door so that no one could walk in on them. Her lips were soft and tender, and their kisses were powerful. His dick throbbed with desire. He could hardly believe that this moment was happening. They broke away from their kiss and she walked over to the back of his desk to get his black leather chair. She wheeled it over to the corner of his office and instructed him to sit down on it. Raul now found himself feeling almost like a student, and the idea that she could be his teacher turned him totally on.

Kathy stood in front of him, seductively moving her hips from side to side, as she stripped out of her clothing. Raul tried hard to control himself. He knew sleeping with a student was wrong, but his dick stood at attention as if it were proud and happy to be in that moment. She got down on her knees in front of the chair and unzipped his pants, releasing his huge cock. Her hands cupped him as she indulged on his thick meat. She gave him some long strokes at first, and then taking hold of his balls, she increased the momentum of her strokes. Her hot wet tongue moved viciously over his dick, and he thought he would lose his mind because of the way she worked her tongue all over him. She took a few minutes to caress the head of his dick, flicking her tongue back and forth on it before giving it a long hard suck. Her hands gently juggled his two balls while her mouth pleasured his dick.

She got back on her feet once more; this time she removed her thin lace underwear and stroked her pussy with her fingers, and then she held those digits out for him to see. Her finger glistened with her wetness, with a locked gaze at him; she slowly brought her wet finger to her lips and sucked it hard. "Umm, delicious," she said as she mounted his dick. Her pussy came crashing down on his dick like a hot volcano. She moved her hips and rode his dick better than any of the girls he had ever fucked in the past. He groaned out, as he took hold of her nipples with his mouth. He licked her nipples and sucked them as she bounced her wet pussy up and down on his hard cock. The more she rode his dick, the hotter they became of each other.

He gripped her ass tightly so that he was controlling her every moment, slamming her body hard against his dick. She moaned in ecstasy and flung her head back as she ground her pussy against his dick. He too was enjoying her and was groaning out in ecstasy. They fucked for what seemed like hours and soon he found himself about to climax. He gave her several hard upward thrusts before exploding his hot cum inside her tight pussy. She gave out a loud moan as she reached the summit of her climax. They took a few minutes to calm down, unable to look each other in the eyes.

Raul could not believe how he had just lost total control of himself. He had been seduced by a twenty-one-year-old student. He finally looked deep into her eyes and realized that she did not have a look of shame in them but rather a look of fulfillment. She had enjoyed their moment of pleasure and was not embarrassed about it. He could not help but be attracted to this girl; he planted a soft kiss on her lips. She welcomed his kiss with her waiting tongue, and they were both distracted by the tapping on the door.

"Are you in there, Raul? We need to talk please," she called out. Raul's eyes popped open as he recognized the voice. It was his ex-girlfriend, Amanda.

10 HIS SENSATIONAL WORKOUTS

The metal bars clanked as Peter let the weights drop unto the purple rug of the Santa Monica Gym. Jennifer, his personal trainer, smiled at him and quickly added that he was in amazing shape.

"Thanks, Jen." He smiled at her as she helped him up. His training had been going well over the past few weeks, and tonight he had decided to treat himself to a few drinks. As he was leaving the gym, he realized that Jennifer was left all alone to pack up all the equipment. He knew that she did not have her car and would have to take the bus at that time of the night. He could not allow her to do that when he had an empty car parked out in the back. His look of admiration for her turned into a look of lust and desire. Her beautiful curly locks bouncing in the air as she rode his dick would be a dream come true for him. Although he hated to admit it, she was a very attractive woman and he longed to be with her in every possible way.

"Hey, what time are you going to leave?" he asked, not realizing that she had headphones in her ears. While waiting for her to respond, his eyes caught sight of the tiny white wire running down from her ears to the side of her sweat pants. He walked up to her and tapped her on the shoulder to get her attention. She responded with a smile as her hazel eyes lit up.

Apparently, she had thought that everyone had already left. His eyes lingered on her sweaty body, and he could see her occasionally glancing down at his scarcely clothed chest. Her sweaty body seemed strangely appealing in the dimly lit gym. The clothes that she wore were very revealing, and he could see her figure clearly. As they stood there, he tried hard to focus on the conversation that they were having, but his mind kept drifting away and visions of her naked kept playing in his mind.

She was shaking nervously and he soon realized that their feelings were mutual. The attraction between them was so intense that he could feel the sexual tension building up in both their bodies. His dick throbbed as he felt the need to make love to her right there in the empty gym. He made the first move and invited her to join him on the judo mat. She happily accepted the invitation, and soon they had locked lips in hot, wet, passionate kiss. She must have had doubts because she pulled away for a second. Peter wasted no time convincing her that what they were doing was right. He swiftly pulled her towards him and gave her a long, deep kiss. She responded by kissing him back with a passion he had never known.

His hand began roaming all over her hot body, stroking it inch by inch. He lifted her sports bra and felt her gasp as he took one full breast in his mouth. He gave her breast a long hard suck, gently flicking his tongue over her nipples. Slowly, he moved his tongue away from her soft melon-shaped breasts and traced his way down to her pants. He unzipped the pants and planted a series of gentle kisses around her navel as she wiggled her legs, trying to get the pants off her. Her skin was beautiful; there were no marks—just smoothness.

Peter enjoyed running his tongue along her skin; she moaned and licked her lips. Finally, he got to the center of her womanhood. Her pussy was clean-shaven: it felt warm and inviting, and he could not resist to taste it. He gently parted her legs, exposing her tender flesh, and took hold of her clitoris with his powerful tongue. He stroked her clitoris with his hot, wet tongue, and when that was not enough, he moved his tongue downwards to her pink flesh, licking and sucking every inch of it. She now moaned louder than before as his tongue ravished her pussy. "I want to feel your tongue in me," she begged.

He gently penetrated the inside of her pussy with his tongue. Her body cringed a little under the pressure, and he had to grip her legs to keep her in position. He now used his tongue to sweep across her pussy. She moaned out loud and he could hear her moans echoing through the empty gym. He now had his fingers making their way down to her wet pussy. Her juices had been flowing freely from the time he had first put his lips down between her legs. She was really enjoying getting her pussy sucked; but "what woman didn't?" he thought as he continued to pleasure her thoroughly. Jennifer's fingers were now running back and forth through his hair. As he sucked her, she could see her body raising the various levels of ecstasy. He wanted to pleasure her, but he did not want her to cum before he could give her every bit of his 8-inch dick. He wanted to rock her insides with his massive cock. He had wanted her from the first time he walked into the gym, and now that he had gotten the opportunity to fuck that pussy, he would not let the chance go to waste.

He pulled his mouth away from her pussy and leaned back, asking her to do him. She knew exactly what he meant because the next thing that he felt was her hot tongue running wildly all over his erect dick. She had several little techniques that she was using to suck his dick. She had something that she did where she used her tongue to trace the veins that ran across his dick from the bottom up. Then, when she got to his purplish head, she licked and flicked her tongue on it. He groaned out in pleasure; every time she licked, he felt the throbbing in his penis intensify and he was not sure how much more of her tongue he would be able to handle. Soon he stopped her for fear that he might come in her mouth and not get the chance to fuck her.

He laid her on her back and mounted her in missionary position, thrusting his cock deep down inside her wet pussy. She moaned out, begging him to fuck her hard. He did exactly what she asked. He gave her several hard thrusts; she moaned hard and cried out in pure ecstasy. Every thrust came with a loud groan, as Peter indulged and allowed desires to control his every movement. In and out his huge cock went, each thrust harder than the last. Jennifer moved in perfect timing with his dick, and the air was filled with her moans. Finally, he gave a long hard thrust and released his hot liquid inside her; she also moaned out loud as he felt tiny spasm from her pussy.

They fell back on the floor and looked at each other in amazement. Peter could not believe that he had just fucked Jennifer right there in the gym.

Peter's girlfriend, Debbie, had just gotten a huge promotion and was hardly ever home. This was one of the main reasons why he had been spending most of his time at the gym. He figured that instead of being out there cheating, he could go to the gym and get a good workout. However, it had seemed like trouble had followed him into the gym when he had fucked his personal trainer. Images of her naked body lying on the floor of the gym kept replaying in his head. He kept hearing the sweet sound of her voice as she moaned out, begging him to fuck her harder.

As he walked into his front door, he was shocked to see that Debbie was already home. The sweet smell of his favorite pecan pie filled the living room. Peter made his way to the kitchen where he was further shocked when his eyes caught hold of Debbie's naked body. She was in the kitchen wearing only a pair of pink stilettos.

"What's going on, Debs," he said as his dick throbbed.

She did not respond right away; instead, she made her way over to him and gave him a hot, passionate kiss that left him feeling dizzy with desire.

"Can't a girl do something nice for her man?" she whispered in his ear, stroking his earlobe with her hot wet tongue.

His heart flipped with joy at the thought of her lying on the kitchen floor naked and covered in whip cream. He cupped her face in his hand and gently kissed her, and his kisses were different from hers: his were soft and tender. He had missed being able to spend time with her.

She pulled out a can of whip cream that she had been hiding behind her back and sprayed some in her mouth, then sprayed some more over her breasts. Then, she made her way out of the kitchen and on to the couch in the living room. Laying on it naked with whip cream on her breast, she gave him a wicked little stare and used her fingers to instruct him to come over to where she was as she sprayed some whip cream over her clean-shaved pussy.

Peter literally leaped across the room. He knelt beside the sofa and began licking off every creamy drop of the whip cream. His tongue stroked her entire body. He got to her nipples and he took the can and sprayed whip cream on them. He licked and sucked each nipple individually, ensuring that he gave each one the proper attention it deserved. Debbie was licking her lips and taking in deep breaths in an effort to control herself. His tongue made its way down to her pussy and lingered there. He sucked her pussy over and over, gently tugging her clit before giving it soft, gentle licks. He could feel his dick throbbing and he wanted to plunge it in so bad, yet he wanted her to be fully satisfied. With him, it was not just all about the sex; he sincerely loved her.

They switched positions so that she was between his legs, sucking him and licking his dick. As she applied the whip cream, her lips followed and she licked it all up. Peter groaned and held onto the back of her head as she pleasured him in a way that had him begging for more. Her tongue took hold of his head, and licked and sucked viciously. She flicked her tongue back and forth on the head and then took the entire dick in her mouth. She almost gagged and he swore that he felt his dick hit the back of her throat. As she continued sucking him, the ecstasy that they felt increased, and so did the momentum of her sucks. She was now sucking him long and hard, and his dick was throbbing with so much intensity that he felt like he would explode in her mouth any time.

"You like this baby?" she said, looking up at him before resuming what she was doing. He barely managed to get an "uh huh" out of his mouth.

Finally, when he could no longer resist the urge, he mounted her and began giving her long hard strokes with his dick. The couch rocked back and forth with the movements that they made on it. Debbie's pussy was incredibly tight, and her hot tongue flicked against his nipples. The harder he thrust his dick inside her, the more she licked and sucked his nipples. With one hard last thrust, he exploded his cum inside her wet pussy; she gave a loud moan and also released her juices. They were both very satisfied, and they cuddled on the couch for a while before heading upstairs to the bedroom for round two.

As Peter lay in bed with his girlfriend that night, he could not help but feel guilty. This was the woman who loved and trusted him, and he had cheated on her. How could he do that to her? What if she were to ever find out about his night of passion with Jennifer at the gym? She would be crushed. He had to put an end to whatever had begun with him and Jennifer before anyone got hurt.

It had been a few weeks since he last went to the gym. Peter wanted to give things time so that it would not be too awkward when he saw

Jennifer. He also wanted to clear the air on a few things; mainly he wanted to let her know that he had a girlfriend and did not intend to ever do what they had done that night again. As he made his way to where Jennifer was working out, he forgot why he had come over. He was now more interested in the way her breasts were bouncing up and down as she ran on the treadmill. She was hot and sweaty just like how she had been on that night; her hair was pulled back in a ponytail and she had her headphones on as usual.

She looked surprised to see him, stating that it had been a while since she saw him and thought he had left the gym or something. He remembered how much fun they used to have, how they would joke around during workouts. Suddenly he felt that there was no need to bring up the past; things seemed pretty much back to normal between them. He looked around and saw that the gym was emptying out. Glancing down at his watch, he saw that it was almost nine, which was their closing time.

"Well, I best be off now," he said to her, as he made his way to the door.

He felt a soft grasp on his hand and looked back to see her walking towards him. She asked him for a ride. Although he wanted to say no because he had honestly feared that they would end up having sex again, he could not find it in himself to allow her to take the bus at this time.

When everyone had left, she began locking up the gym. He sat on one of the chairs, waiting for her. As she emerged out from the almost dark gym, he was once again smitten by her beauty. It felt like he was in a trance. As he stood up, his lips met hers, and once again, they were passionately kissing each other at the gym. This time it seemed like he had missed her because his kisses had more desire in them. Their hands ran all over each other's bodies, and soon they were undressing each other. As her clothes fell to the floor, he took her into his arms and braced her up against one of the machines. He bent her over with her ass jutting upward.

She looked so beautiful in that position: her ass had a perfect round shape, and he could not resist the urge to give her several hard smacks across it. As he smacked her, she whispered that she liked it and wanted him to smack her ass again. He fulfilled her desire and smacked her harder a few more times. She moaned and he felt like it would explode with desire. He parted her ass cheeks and entered her pussy from the back. Her pussy was hot and wet, yet it was quite tight and he had a little difficulty thrusting his dick all the way inside. He did not quite understand; he had fucked her few weeks ago and felt this tightness, but now it felt even tighter than before. Was it all a figment of his imagination, his desire to fuck getting the best of him? He did not know, but he closed his eyes as he gripped onto her ass, thrusting his dick inside her tiny pussy several times.

"Oh yeah, fuck, yeah, harder, baby, yeah," he heard her cry.

He continued to penetrate her insides. He could now hear the sound of his balls hitting hard against her flesh as he slammed his long dick inside her. Her juices oozed out of her sweet pussy, and in that moment, if he had to choose between her and his girlfriend, he would have definitely chosen her. There was just something about this woman that he loved. Suddenly he stopped; unable to believe his ears, had she really asked him to fuck her in the ass? Somehow, women tended to shy away from anal sex with him, saying that it hurt too much. Yet Jennifer had begged for that to be done to her. It was a plea he could not resist.

He pulled his dick out of her wet pussy and used some of her wetness to lubricate her anus. Then, he used some of his saliva to lubricate his dick, rubbing it thoroughly over his full length. He gently spread her ass cheeks and found her anus with the tip of his cock. Slowly, he penetrated inside her asshole. Her body tensed up and she clenched her teeth as he pushed his dick deeper and deeper inside her. Finally, when it was fully inside, he began stroking her anus with his dick. He gave her slow gentle thrusts at first. Her anus was even tighter than her pussy; in fact, it was the tightest hole his dick had ever penetrated. As he fucked her, she cried out; he could not quite make out whether it was from the pleasure or from the pain. However, he did not stop—she was the one who had asked him to fuck her ass and that's exactly what he was going to give to her. Without stopping, he penetrated her asshole over and over. Each time his dick made its way inside her tightness, she moaned and cried. He was getting a thrill from the way she was moaning and how tight her hole had been. He increased his momentum and gave her some long, hard strokes, followed by quicker, harder strokes. He was panting heavily as he felt his blood rushing down to his dick. Harder and harder, he thrust until he gave her one last hard thrust and exploded his hot cum inside her ass. She moaned out as she too reached her own climax.

They sat in the gym for a while just watching each other with smiles on their faces as they calmed down from their moment of pleasure. As he sat there, his phone rang; it was Debbie. Reality set in and Peter realized that once again, he had found himself having a different type of workout at the gym. It was amazing how he had come with one thing on his mind—to end things with Jennifer—yet he was leaving having done the complete opposite of what he had come to do. Jennifer looked at him, hot and sweaty, then leaned in to whisper in his ear, "Wow, what a sensational workout." He looked at her in the corner of his eyes as a wicked smile swept across his face. He had to admit fucking Jennifer was quite a workout.

AUTHOR'S NOTE

Readers: I want to expand a few of the stories to see where the characters can be explored further. If there are any of the stories that you would like to read more about again, I'd love to hear from you!

Visit my blog at www.shalabreece.com

Join my newsletter for free exclusive previews
http://www.shalabreece.com/in

Follow me on Twitter at
http://www.twitter.com/shalabreece

Like my page on Facebook at
http://www.facebook.com/shalabreece

Discover my books at major ebook retailers everywhere.